E/+ 8/85

THE MASS OF THE GALAXY WAS BEHIND THEM . . .

Pete ran a star search and found something else. Something nearby. He pushed the button to activate the search screen, expected to see *Rimfire*, huge, majestic. He saw instead a Blink Beacon.

The contents of the Beacon's tape made only a small disturbance on the surface of his ship's tape. He tinkered with it, found the frequencies it responded to, and then he was digesting some startling figures.

Just under a thousand years ago, a fleet had passed the Beacon. And then there was nothing until, loud and clear, there came a pre-blink signal which was recorded to indicate that the blinking ship had skipped past the Beacon, flying through subspace outward toward total blackness.

Jan and Pete looked outward toward emptiness and shivered. "*Rimfire* went past," Jan said. "Out there . . ."

GOLD STAR

Great Science Fiction from SIGNET

(0451)

- ☐ **THE SLEEPING DRAGON: Guardians of the Flame #1 by Joel Rosenberg.** (125746—$2.95)*
- ☐ **WIZARDS: Isaac Asimov's Magical Worlds of Fantasy #1 edited by Isaac Asimov, Martin H. Greenberg and Charles G. Waugh.** (125428—$3.50)*
- ☐ **LAST COMMUNION by Nicholas Yermakov.** (098226—$2.25)
- ☐ **EPIPHANY by Nicholas Yermakov.** (118847—$2.50)*
- ☐ **THOSE WHO WATCH by Robert Silverberg.** (120221—$2.25)*
- ☐ **STRATA by Terry Pratchett.** (121473—$2.75)*
- ☐ **THOSE WHO CAN by Robin Scott Wilson.** (615956—$1.95)
- ☐ **GREYBEARD by Brian Aldiss.** (090357—$1.75)*
- ☐ **WIND CHILD by R. M. Meluch.** (115287—$2.50)
- ☐ **WIND DANCERS by R. M. Meluch.** (097866—$2.25)
- ☐ **THUNDERWORLD by Zach Hughes.** (112903—$2.25)*

*Prices slightly higher in Canada.

Buy them at your local bookstore or use this convenient coupon for ordering.

THE NEW AMERICAN LIBRARY, INC.,
P.O. Box 999, Bergenfield, New Jersey 07621

Please send me the books I have checked above. I am enclosing $________
(please add $1.00 to this order to cover postage and handling). Send check or money order—no cash or C.O.D.'s. Prices and numbers are subject to change without notice.

Name____________________

Address____________________

City __________ State __________ Zip Code __________

Allow 4-6 weeks for delivery.
This offer is subject to withdrawal without notice.

GOLD STAR

by

Zach Hughes

A SIGNET BOOK
NEW AMERICAN LIBRARY
TIMES MIRROR

NAL BOOKS ARE AVAILABLE AT QUANTITY DISCOUNTS WHEN USED TO PROMOTE PRODUCTS OR SERVICES. FOR INFORMATION PLEASE WRITE TO PREMIUM MARKETING DIVISION, THE NEW AMERICAN LIBRARY, INC., 1633 BROADWAY, NEW YORK, NEW YORK 10019.

Copyright © 1983 by Hugh Zachary

All rights reserved

SIGNET TRADEMARK REG. U.S. PAT. OFF. AND FOREIGN COUNTRIES
REGISTERED TRADEMARK—MARCA REGISTRADA
HECHO EN CHICAGO, U.S.A.

SIGNET, SIGNET CLASSIC, MENTOR, PLUME, MERIDIAN AND NAL BOOKS are published by The New American Library, Inc.,
1633 Broadway, New York, New York 10019

First Printing, December, 1983

1 2 3 4 5 6 7 8 9

PRINTED IN THE UNITED STATES OF AMERICA

1

Peter Jaynes came from deep sleep into instant alertness. He lay on his back, his eyes looking upward toward the planetside landscape which Jan had programmed into the decopanel on the bulkhead over the bed. The subconscious memory of a sound was just beyond his reach. He lifted his head from the pillow, was very still. The only thing he heard was Jan's deep, even breathing. He sighed, let his neck relax, and put out his hand to the heated softness of a rounded hip.

He decided that he'd dreamed a sound. He turned and put one arm across Jan. She slept in the same garment she'd been wearing during the last wake period, a silken singlet. There was no need for formality on a deep-space tug crewed by man and wife.

The tantalizing near-memory of having been awakened by something continued to nag at him. He closed his eyes but did not feel sleepy. He turned onto his back again. The landscape overhead had changed to show a Tigian sky over hard, red, rocky hills. It had rained and a rainbow arced the dome of blue. He was not going to be able to get back to sleep.

"Come on, legs," he said aloud. Legs heard and obeyed, swung off the bed. Jan stirred, but did not awaken. He checked the wall chronometer. He was only halfway through the sleep period, which accounted for his slight feeling of grogginess.

He stepped into the shower. Cold, stinging, refreshing water penetrated the singlet he wore. He shook his head and sent droplets flying, cut off the water, stood with his eyes closed as a warm breeze from an ecologically pure desert dried him.

The *Stranden 47*, Mule Class space tug, registered out of New Earth, was over two hundred light-years from the nearest populated planet. You didn't just ignore sounds, sounds so unusual that they woke you up, when you were that far from nowhere.

A deep-space blink ship of any class was no place for odd sounds. Aboard any blinker things hummed, purred, clicked, bleeped, whistled, but each sound indicated perfect order, perfectly functioning hardware. An unusual sound usually meant that something had gone wrong in one of a couple of hundred thousand servomechanisms. A Mule Class tug had backup systems for backup systems, but the loss of any one system was a potentially serious threat which, if unattended, could make it doubtful that you'd ever get back to anywhere to collect deep-space bonus pay.

Peter examined his face in the mirror as he brushed his hair. He saw a regular, not exactly ugly fellow who stood compactly just under six feet, with a strong neck, a thick chest, and well-muscled arms and torso. He was beginning to feel good. He'd run ship's gravity up to Earth Standard plus 0.1 because Jan had gained three pounds in the past thirty days. The extra exertion required by the additional 0.1 gravity would use up enough calories to trim her down.

The logical place to start an inspection tour was the power room. The generator was on full charge with all readings normal. The power of the generator field made the blond hair stand up on his head and try to separate into individual strands. It was not a bad feeling. It was a healthy, reassuring tingle. There under the circular shield was the thing which gave deep-space wings to man, the blink generator. The *Stranden 47*'s generator was a real horse, hefty enough to send the relatively small tug several galaxies away in one blink if the coordinates had been available, powerful enough to allow the *47* to latch onto the largest liner or freighter and blink her to the nearest repair base.

No one really knew the potential power which was stored in even the smallest blink generator. It had been said that not even Billy Bob Blink, the Texan who had developed the blink generator, fully understood what happened when the energy accumulated in a blink generator was released. The practical result was that anything attached to the generator's vehicle or within the generated field ceased to exist in one location and came to exist in another.

Pete worked his way through a checklist. There was nothing amiss. The generator was always held at full charge so that the *47* was ready to blink on a moment's notice in the event of a distress call. Such a call could come from the four directions of the blink routes which intersected at the *47*'s station.

There wasn't all that much more to inspect once he had finished the power-room checklist. The generator took up a full half of the ship's 150-foot length.

The compact control room, one wall taken up by the communications equipment, was located next to the power room. Aside from a tool and supply storage area the remaining space inside *Stranden 47*'s rectangular, rounded-cornered hull was living area for a four-man crew. With only two people aboard, the living area was ample to luxurious. Into that space, roughly seventy-five by fifty feet, the Stranden designers had packed the food-preparation and dining areas, a small swimming pool which served as storage for the bulk of the ship's constantly recycled water, an exercise room, two lounge rooms, and two bedrooms. The Mule Class was designed to house a crew of four. Each time a Mule put out into deep space she was stocked with food and supplies for four. Pete and Jan Jaynes had food and some luxuries to last for twice the period of their contracted tour, because it was often difficult to find even two crewmen to man a deep-space tug. It was lonely work.

Pete checked instruments in the control room. The *47* was in a good mood. She hummed at him and blinked reassuring little lights at him, and her computer gave him a quick readout which said "great" for all systems. He was becoming more and more convinced that he'd dreamed the sound. Not only were all primary systems great, all backup systems and secondary backup systems were great. A Mule Class tug stayed in space for a long time.

At times of emergency, great demands were made on a tug. A Mule was known to be the most dependable vessel ever sent into space.

Pete had saved the communications board for last. There were only two possible communications signals which would have activated any sound-producing mechanism on the *47*. He pushed the self-examination button on the communications board and watched as the ship's computer showed blinking green after blinking green.

There was a gong mounted in each separate ship's area, a gong which went bonkers upon activation by the communications board. When the gongs echoed throughout the ship it meant one of two things: Either a Blinkstat directed to the *47* was coming in or the detection equipment had sensed the pre-arrival signal of a blinking ship. If either of those things had happened the gongs would still have been bonging.

The signal-indicator light was off. No Blinkstat, no call, no pre-arrival signal had come into the big bank of electronics.

Pete sat down in the padded command chair and stared at nothing. He felt, rather than heard, Jan come into control. They were that close. He sensed her presence, turned, winked at her.

"It's the middle of the night," she said sleepily.

Lord, Lord, he thought. Just seeing her was a pleasure of which he would never tire. She was so beautiful, so rounded in the right places. She looked to him more the Tri-D star than a crewman on a tug. The silken singlet molded itself to her. She came to lean her hip against his shoulder. He felt the warmth of her, allowed himself the luxury of a touch, smoothed his hand over the silkiness.

"Coming back to bed?" she asked.

"I don't know. I guess."

"What woke you?"

"I don't know. A dream."

She sat down in the other command chair, turned it on its swivels to face him. "Was your dream something like a signal gong going off?" Her steel-gray eyes were on his.

He felt a little shiver go up his back. "You heard something, too?"

"I'm not sure. I'm like you. I could have dreamed it."

"Honey, I love you, but when we start to dream the same dreams at the same time I'm going to wonder if such closeness is possible."

Pete pushed buttons. Since the incoming-signal light was not on he had not checked the tape for the sleeptime period. He put the audio on high-speed search and there was a whirr of sound and a hum of motion and then a little click and there it was.

The sound was weak and incomplete. The tone, however, was that of the warning gong. The sound lasted a fraction of a second and then was gone. He played it back four times, then did a high-speed search of the entire four hours of tape.

There was only the momentary hint of sound, almost a ghost of a sound. He turned the problem over to the computer and had an analysis in seconds. The sound had the tonal qualities of the communications warning gong. It lasted microseconds. The signal which had activated the gong for that brief moment, so brief it had not reached standard volume, had come from that section of the detection equipment which searched for the pre-arrival signal of a blinking ship.

"Just a glitch," Jan said. "A ghost."

"It came from Number One," Pete said. For brevity, they had numbered the four intersecting blink routes so that in referring to them they would not have to use the full, lengthy chart designations.

It worried him. A tiny microsecond signal had come through the far reaches of empty space which stretched back and away down the blink ranges toward home.

Only one thing in the universe was known to be faster than the instantaneous travel of a blinking ship. Perhaps more research had been done on that phenomenon than on any other aspect of the blink mystery. A blinking ship sends a signal ahead of itself. The signal is unlike any known emission. As far as man knew, that particular signal, that flash sent toward the emergence point at the moment of generator activation, had not existed prior to the first use of Billy Bob Blink's machine. The pre-arrival signal could be detected along the entire length of the projected jump.

The pre-arrival signal worried some. The space services spent millions each year trying to determine the cause of it, trying to find a way to eliminate it, for, although microseconds were involved, the pre-arrival signal gave electronic equipment time to prepare for the actual arrival of the ship. There hadn't been a war for almost a thousand years, but to the military mind that warning that a ship was on its way was, potentially, a dangerous situation.

"Just a glitch," Jan said. "Let's go back to bed."

"You go along. I'll be there in a few minutes."

She didn't have to use words to let him know that she was not going without him. They had been together for three years. In that three years the longest period of separation had been two hours, when she was taking her physical for tug duty. Even then Pete had tried to go into the examination room with her. He had just found her, then, and he was afraid of losing her.

When Pete Jaynes worried, his left hand went to his head. If he was wearing a cap at the time the fingers of his left hand would slip under the cap, tilting it, until the pads of his index and large fingers were on the depression in his skull just over his left ear. If he was not wearing a cap the motion seemed less unconscious. Jan saw his hand go up, begin to toy with the dent in his skull.

"Pete, it was a false signal. There's no need to worry."

Pete knew that Jan had not spent almost a full year of two-hour-a-day classes studying shipboard communications equipment. Jan could not know that what had happened was impossible, that the signal of a blinking ship could not emerge out of empty space. The signal had been recorded. Weak as it was, momentary as it was, it was there. It had been automatically transcribed from the communicator tape to the master tape. At the end of the tour that master tape would have three full years of ship's functions recorded on it, and it would be run routinely through the Stranden Corporation's statistical information center. Any operator could review any category of information with the press of a button. Stranden was, of course, under the jurisdiction of the Space Service, and any Space Service statistician had access to Stranden's records, could press a button and review, for example, all of the incoming jump signals on the tape within seconds.

The weak, momentary signal was there on tape. For the skipper of any spacegoing ship to ignore such a signal, which without a doubt indicated something abnormal, was, at the least, grounds for losing one's license.

The master tape of the *Stranden 47* would be easy to review, because Pete had deliberately chosen an isolated, seldom-visited outpost in nowhere. There wouldn't be many signals of any sort in the three years of their duty there.

Pete liked tug duty. At first he'd been concerned about Jan's reaction to prolonged isolation. Theirs, as the trite old saying went, was not exactly a marriage made in heaven. He had had one hell of a time persuading her to marry him. The first time he saw her in the Spacer's Rest on Tigian she'd called him a loser. He didn't deny it, but he did have enough self-image to go back. He paid the usual exorbitant prices charged by such places as the Spacer's Rest just to spend time with her. What he did with that time surprised Jan. He used the time for talking. That was not what she was usually paid to do. The Spacer's Rest, tastefully furnished, serving the finest foods from a hundred planets, was not a place for rest and relaxation. It was a whorehouse.

Pete looked back on those nights in the Spacer's Rest now and then with a certain nostalgia. There they were, one loser with a hole in his head, a dent in his skull, some brain cells forever destroyed by the injury, just enough to ruin hell out of Peter Jaynes deductive reasoning. Without that ability, passing the exams in his last year at the Academy was impossible. The Academy was sorry as all hell, for, after all, the injury to Pete's brain had come as the result of school activity. An escape hatch had blown on the training ship, and the resulting explosive decompression had sent Cadet Jaynes into space, with a quick blow to the head as he passed through the hatch. They said he was lucky. He was in space with air leaking from his ruptured helmet.

Well, perhaps, he admitted, he was lucky to be alive, to have been picked up before the pressure inside the suit was low enough to boil his blood. And everyone was sorry as hell that the Service demanded that a space officer have all his brains. You just didn't fly a sleek fleet liner, or a fleet freighter, much less an X&A Explorer Class or a ship of the line if a little chunk of brain didn't function.

But there was another loser at the Spacer's Rest. She was a tall, blond, female loser, a New Earther a long way from home. She had worked hard to save the fare out to Tigian in order to study art on that planet most famous for its artists. She had butted nose-on into Tigian snobbery. To a Tigian, there was no such thing as a non-Tigian artist.

A work permit? Sorry, it just wasn't done. Non-Tigians were not issued work permits. A way home? Sorry. The fleet had just been put under a new directive. There would be no more casuals aboard ship. Too many fleet officers had been taking advantage of the system, which had allowed working passage to selected individuals. Most of the selected individuals were, it seemed, rather attractive girls, many of them on holiday from such places as the Spacer's Rest on Tigian. It wasn't good for morale for the officers to have their own private women on board. All fleet employees, even casual, had to have at least two years of space training at an accredited institution.

So what does a girl do when she's light-years from home, broke, unable to get a job to earn passage back to New Earth? Does she just give up, lie down, and starve? No. She lies down, but not to starve.

"At least," Jan had told Peter Jaynes, after about four nights of his nonstop attempt to convince her that tug duty was not all bad, "they've eradicated all the things that used to be called social diseases."

Tigian was an odd planet. Tigians were artists, and, therefore, a bit more liberal than most. On Tigian, whores were often invited to the best parties. It was a good living, and she was meeting some interesting people.

Before Pete could get her to marry him he had to remind her of her New Earth upbringing, of the morality with which she'd been instilled as a young girl. He had to make her weep.

They were together. Jan, being fairly new at her occupation, didn't know much about spacers. She knew only that they seemed to have money to burn when they were at the Spacer's Rest. She didn't know that in wooing her, Pete had spent most of the earnings from his last tour on a tug. She didn't know that the fine, spacious apartment where they honeymooned had been rented with an advance on Pete's next tour. When Pete came in with a one-way ticket for one to New Earth she wept for the second time since she'd known him.

"It's the only way, honey," he'd told her.

"You're asking me to go back to New Earth and wait? Wait for three years?"

"I have to go back to work. We're broke. There's

enough to get you home and give you living money until I can have the company send you more."

Pete had learned, then, the sort of woman he'd married. "I will not allow you to leave me," she'd said. "You will not dump me somewhere for three years, damn you, just when I'm getting to like being with you."

At that time there were things about Jan that Pete didn't know. He didn't know that she'd come to dislike all men. Her idea of heaven was to be alone, totally alone, forever alone, never to be touched, never to hear a man's voice.

She had joined with a loser for one reason—to get out of the Spacer's Rest. She'd agreed to marry Pete because, in her mind, having just one man touch her was preferable, but only slightly, to being touched by any man with the money in his pocket. Then she fell in love with this loser, and loved being touched by him, and he was going to ship her light-years away and go light-years away in the other direction and leave her alone for three years.

"They take female crew on tugs," she said. "I know they do. I've met women who work tugs."

The problem was that she had no experience. She had only a liberal-arts degree. She had been in space just once, the jump from New Earth to Tigian. Her technical ability was limited to knowing how to turn on the lights and music in the rented apartment. Pete didn't have much hope, but he liked the idea. If she thought she dreaded being away from him for three years, she should have been able to get inside his head and see the bleak, painful darkness which was growing there with just the thought of having to say goodbye to her.

He found his personal heaven in the office of the

procurement officer of the Stranden Corporation. Stranden was one of several tug companies operating off Tigian. It was not one of the leading companies. All tug men knew companies like Stranden, and, if they had a choice, worked for the big, glamour companies that furnished deep-space tug service along the most-traveled routes. All stations on all blink routes were allocated by bid, and the big companies could afford to bid high for the highly traveled routes because more traffic meant more ship breakdowns and more salvage money.

Stranden Corporation's salvage record was terrible, because it was a low bidder on routes and stations so isolated, so little traveled, that the chance of a tug's getting a Lloyd's contract on a disabled ship were near zero. The big, prosperous companies didn't even bother to bid on stations such as the one occupied by the *Stranden 47*, or if they did, they bid so high that there wasn't a chance of getting the station.

Most men went into tug service for two reasons—steady money and the hope, the chance, for big money. Tugs were free enterprise. The system was a holdover from thousands of years into the past of old Earth. Because of the long tours and the smallness of the tugs, because Space Service fleet ships were huge and luxurious and put into port often, the service got the cream of the spacegoing crop from each planet. Like the system itself, tug men were throwbacks.

Tug men were often independent, not fond of taking orders. Some drank, lived for the months between tours. They earned good money, even if they didn't get to participate in a rescue or salvage operation, and they spent it in one continuous spree of drinking and women. Some tug men were rejects.

Peter Jaynes fell into that category. To a smartly dressed member of the Space Service, freshly off a luxurious fleet liner, all tug men were weird. The weirdest of them signed three-year contracts with the fringe companies such as Stranden.

Stranden's Mule Class tugs were safe, dependable, serviceable. They were old, however. Many of the Stranden's tugs had been phased out by the companies that could afford the new equipment, could afford to bid low enough to get the highly traveled stations.

Those men and women who made careers of spending years at a time on a stationary ship at some designated pinpoint deep in space could pick and choose. They chose the companies with the best equipment and the best chance of salvage-money bonuses. Most companies, for example, had home-planet transmission of entertainment programs aboard their tugs. Stranden had only a film library.

The quality of the entertainment didn't concern two losers. They had found each other. When Pete and Jan were dropped off to relieve the two-man crew of the *Stranden 47*, they spent the first six months just getting acquainted. Pete was glad it was an inactive post. He had gone into tug work with the idea that maybe he'd luck out and get a crewman's share of a big Lloyd's contract, maybe a freighter loaded with diamonds. He'd been aboard one tug which blinked a disabled, antique training ship back to the repair shops, and his share of the salvage money had been almost a quarter of his salary for the two-year tour, but he'd never hit the jackpot. Now he didn't care. He had all the treasure he would ever want. He had the universe in his arms each night.

Pete was pleased in many ways. *Stranden 47* was his first command. He took orders from no one. He was pleased when, in the first year, the total traffic handled by the *47* was one Blinkstat to be forwarded from a distant X&A ship toward New Earth Headquarters. He was more than content to have the *47* sit there in her designated spot, close by a blink beacon, for the rest of the tour. He had Jan. Two losers had won big. Two lonely people had discovered each other, and had found, in each other, the key element needed for individual personal completion.

Rather spoiled by the inactivity, Pete resented the intrusion of the unexplained, weak, ghostly signal. He fingered the dent in his skull and worried about it. He looked forward to many more tours with Jan. But the tape had recorded a signal, a blink signal. It had come from down the New Earth range.

"It's all right," he told Jan, with a wry grin, when she told him to quit worrying. "I've lost my power of deductive reason, so I can't worry as deeply as most men can."

"That's not true," she said.

"It's impossible," he said.

"It was a glitch."

"It is impossible for the signal to be on the tape," he said slowly, "unless, one, a ship sent it, or two, something happened to a ship at the beginning of a blink."

"Or three," she said, "unless the equipment just hiccuped."

Pete had the training to repair non-major malfunctions. He began to review in his mind the procedure for testing the communications bank. It was a massive undertaking for one man. He'd be finished with it, maybe, just in time for the relief crew. In the event of a malfunction which he was unable to repair, he was required to report via Blinkstat to the home office on Tigian. A tug without communications is useless. If he reported the signal, and still couldn't account for its origin, they might have to take the ship back to Tigian before the end of his tour. In that case, there'd be financial penalties. They would lose all accrued bonus pay.

There had been cases when a crew, with dissension aboard, would deliberately sabotage a vital piece of equipment so that a relief tug would be sent out and the unhappy crew could take their tug back to planetside. All such events were investigated thoroughly.

So, Pete was thinking, what if he called home and they said bring her in for an overhaul and some smart joker at Stranden decided that there'd been no malfunction, or if there had been that a crew not composed of losers such as an Academy kick-out and an ex-hooker could have repaired it? What if Stranden decided that the man-wife team of Pete and Jan Jaynes couldn't cut it on a tug?

Now that was something to worry about. Even if he could find another tug job, that would be the end of heaven. He would not risk losing the coming years of the joy of being alone with her without exploring all possibilities. This was a trial tour for the Jayneses, and he wasn't going to blow it because of some glitch in an electronic system.

And yet he worried. His woman stood beside him, her hip against his shoulder, and she hurt inside to see the pained look on his face. She'd told him time and time again that there wasn't a thing wrong with his mind, not with his deductive reasoning or anything else. But he knew. He was the one who had failed the tests during his last year at the Academy. He was the one who had begged the people at Stranden to take on an inexperienced woman.

"Pete," she whispered, putting her hand atop his to stop his fingers from their continuous examination of the dent in his skull. "Pete, now you stop it."

"You're right," he said.

"I'm always right," she said, with a little smile.

"It's time to stop worrying and start doing something."

"What?"

He didn't answer. He swiveled his chair to the control panel, punched up the blink beacon guide on the screen, and made his selection, his fingers flying over the keyboard.

"Hang on, honey," he said.

Moving a Mule Class tug was a joy. There was power to waste. Blinks came fast and easy. Not even a fleet liner could build charge for a blink as fast as that huge power plant down there on one end of the *47*'s rectangular hull.

As Pete activated the brute power of the generator there was a feeling of displacement, a tingling unlike anything ever experienced, a wrenching feeling of movement which was not movement and ended almost before it began.

The hardware blinked, clicked, hummed, sensing a new starfield around the ship, orienting the ship instantly and giving exact coordinates. Pete put the viewer on telescopic scan and located the blink beacon which had been his target. It had been a long jump. The blink beacon on the New Earth range was the nearest beacon to the *47*'s permanent station.

Even without deductive reasoning, Pete had guessed that if the signal which was worrying him had been genuine, and not just a glitch in the equipment aboard his ship, it might also be recorded on the permanent tape of the New Earth range beacons.

There was a new feeling inside the *47*. The generator was reaching out, building charge, and the result was that special feeling of tingling power. There near the fringe of the galaxy the distance between beacons was great, measured not in light-years but in parsecs. The star fields were thin, scattered. The blink had taken power, and now the generator was drawing on the stars to rebuild.

Pete ran a check, got a "great" reading from the computer. The blink beacon, within optical distance, sent out its steady, perpetual target signal. He punched instructions into the keyboard which activated a system and pulled the readings from the beacon's tapes. The action recorded the *47*'s name, the time, the date on the beacon's tape.

He saw that the beacon's tape had not been monitored in the past five years, a testimony to the remoteness of the range. He started a fast search of the tape. Two ships had passed the beacon in five years and then the reading was up-to-date, and, at the precise time recorded by the *47*'s computer there was, on the beacon's tape, that same ghostly signal. The computer analyzed and said the two readings were identical. Weak, incomplete, but the signal definitely was the beginning of that signal which a blinking ship sends ahead of itself through the continuum.

He ran stress and wave analysis a second time, and the results were the same. His ship's communications bank and the blink beacon had recorded the signal at the same time.

Jan's face had gone serious. She sat in her command chair and watched Pete play with the computer, running the two signals through for comparison again and again. She was silent. She knew him well now, and she knew that when he was doing serious thinking he didn't like to be distracted.

He punched instructions, and the two tapes played together. Then he began to slow the speed of play, and the sound changed tones, but began to be stretched out. They both heard the difference in the two tapes at the same time when Pete had the momentary sound stretched out for a full ten seconds.

The tape of the blink beacon had recorded something which was not on *Stranden 47*'s tape. That additional something was not signal. It was more a distortion of the coating of the tape.

"Defect in manufacture?" Pete muttered, running the two sounds again. "No," he said, in answer to his own question.

He had Jan dig out a technical manual and bent over it for a few minutes.

"Find anything?" Jan asked when he looked up.

"I don't know," he said. "It may have been an emission of a kind of energy which the tape was not designed to print."

"So?" she asked.

"I'd like to check the next beacon down the New Earth range."

"Ummm," she said. It was not up to her to remind him that he'd defied company and Space Service policy by leaving station without first Blink-stating his intentions to the home office. She knew that he was taking a chance that there would be no traffic through their remote junction of space routes during the few minutes it took to blink out and check the blink beacon's tape and then blink back home.

The generator's charge was building to a power which caused Jan's hair to tend to stand out straight. Her skin tingled. She had a thought which sent a smile to warm her face. Making love during a generator charge was, well, it was just wow.

Pete began to punch the coordinates for the jump back to the station. He'd decided that it was too risky to blink farther away from his assigned place to check another beacon's tape. He was about ready to call the home office and lay it all in their laps. He jerked with surprise, and Jan gave a small cry, when the communicator began to blink lights at them and the golden tone of the gong filled the control room.

Pete whirled his chair to the communications bank and monitored. The nearby blink beacon was relaying a Blinkstat. The coded signal came into the ship's communications bank and from there was transcribed into the odd, mechanical voice of the ship's computer. At the same time a printer was working with a chatter.

"X&A, New Earth, to *U.P.S. Rimfire*. Order: immediate contact."

That was it. The message was from Exploration and Alien Search Headquarters, New Earth.

Blinkstats, which were possible through the same power that lifted a ship from one point to another instantaneously, followed a line of pre-established blink beacons. Blinkstats were expensive. When the ship for which a Blinkstat was intended received the message, the expensive transmission was terminated by automatics at the next blink beacon past the ship's position.

Even a man without deductive reasoning could figure out that the *U.P.S. Rimfire* was thought by X&A to be on the New Earth range leading toward the *Stranden 47*'s station. Since the message had arrived at the blink beacon near the *47*'s present location, *Rimfire* had to be somewhere between that blink beacon and the next one downrange toward New Earth.

Pete sent a test signal down the New Earth range toward the home planet, with programmed termination at a selected beacon far away. Each of the beacons which he tested had relayed the Blinkstat intended for *Rimfire*. He punched other instructions and found that the beacon nearest him had relayed the stat on to the beacon at his home station, and that beacon, too, had relayed.

Pete was beginning to have a creepy feeling. There was no way that the newest and most glamorous ship in the service of Exploration and Alien Search could have passed the *Stranden 47*'s station. Not unless X&A and the service had come up with something so new that all of the old rules were out. He didn't think it possible that such a development had been made.

Even before she was ready to go into space the *U.P.S. Rimfire* had been a famous ship. She had been undergoing final outfitting at the time Pete and Jan left Tigian to begin their tour. The media had been full of her. She was the first X&A ship with true intergalactic capability. She was the finest and most expensive ship ever built. According to Tigian Tri-D, not always dependable, considering the Tigian temperament, *Rimfire*'s skipper was to be given the order to take the *Rimfire* toward the fringe stars, to the last established blink beacon, and turn left.

There was no way she could be out there beyond the *47*'s station.

Pete punched in the buttons for home, felt the leap, and the old *47* was back within fractions of an inch of her original position at the junction of four lonely blink routes leading from nowhere to nothing. The homebase blink beacon had dutifully recorded the Blinkstat for *Rimfire* and relayed it.

Pete was glumly silent for a long time.

"Hungry?" Jan asked.

"Not very."

"Bowl of kanji fruit?"

"Sounds good."

She started to rise, and the tone of his voice stopped her. She settled back.

"What we're gonna hear, and pretty soon, is an all-points alert on *Rimfire*," he said.

"Oh, no," Jan said.

"Let's eat," he said. "It'll take a while."

It took twelve hours. The Blinkstat came from New Earth, and it was a blockbuster, carrying the preliminary code which indicated that it was being sent simultaneously along all established blink routes. The general transmission, in itself, was a tipoff to the seriousness of the situation, even if the wording was not. The message was merely a formal request to all ships in space, all stations, all fleet installations to report any knowledge of *U.P.S. Rimfire*.

It was when the stat gave *Rimfire*'s last known position that Pete began to dream. *Rimfire*'s arrival had been recorded at blink beacon 7C3X99-34R-

NE793. Her next jump should have been recorded at blink beacon 7C3X99-34R-NE794.

"NE794," Pete muttered.

"That's where we went," Jan said.

"She arrived at NE793." Now he was beginning to regret that he hadn't had more courage, that he had not jumped on downrange to NE793.

"She's lost," he said.

She was the most expensive ship ever built. She had every piece of equipment known to man. She could chart new routes in space, discover new planets; she had on board the equipment to analyze every aspect of that new planet and, in the unlikely event of life, hostile life, she was armed with weapons which could reduce a world to charred cinders in seconds.

Pete couldn't even estimate her worth, but he had a glowing feeling as his dream grew. The crew's share of a salvage on *Rimfire* would be the single biggest haul ever made. He started punching buttons. He wouldn't reveal the dream to Jan. Not yet. No use raising her hopes until he had a more solid handle on the situation.

But *Rimfire* was lost. Out there between the *47* and the first beacon down the New Earth range were a few parsecs of empty space. Past that one, NE 794, a few more parsecs, and *Rimfire*'s last known position near NE793.

"Jan," he said, "send a stat to Stranden on Tigian. Keep it simple. Just say *Stranden 47* asks permission begin search *Rimfire*."

Jan had learned fast. Her fingers flew over the keyboard. The tiny amount of energy required to send a signal allowed almost instantaneous relay down the Tigian range. The answer was clicking off the printer within a minute.

"They say hold," Jan said. "Must confirm *Rimfire* in trouble."

Pete used one of his infrequent profanities, then shook his head. "If she wasn't in trouble she wouldn't have disappeared."

If it was simple trouble, such as merely falling out of blink drive before arriving at NE 794, somewhere in those parsecs of empty space between beacons, her communications generator was enough to send a call for help. Pete knew the space regulations. No skipper would be silent if his ship was in trouble. If he had a way to yell for help, he'd be yelling loud and clear. If anyone was alive on *Rimfire* and if the communications equipment was working, there'd be a call going both ways down the New Earth range.

The blink was a relatively safe way to travel, but when man depends on hardware and electronics, he is vulnerable. Hardware and electronics fail. The results, to a blink ship, are not always tragic, or fatal. Sometimes a generator just lost power for one reason or another and dropped the ship out of subspace, or wherever a ship went when blinking, back into normal space a long, long way from anywhere.

There were no mysteries in space travel. When a ship failed to arrive, and didn't report, a search always found her. There'd been a few times when the search found a dead ship, gutted by internal explosion, but even the dead ships were found. There were some old stories from the last war, a thousand years old, about ships disappearing, but that was war. It's difficult to find the disassembled atoms of a ship which has been caught in the full blast of a rebinder beam.

Pete's guess was that whatever had happened to *Rimfire*, it was damned serious. It saddened him. He'd never seen her, but he'd seen pictures of her, and she was one beautiful hunk of stuff.

"Jan, she's lost all power. If she had auxiliary power we'd be hearing from her. She's out there somewhere between 794 and 793." He didn't add that there might be people still alive on her, people who were waiting and praying for a tug.

He made up his mind. "Send this to Stranden. *Stranden 47* blinking NE794 to begin search."

He didn't bother to wait for an answer. The *47* ceased to exist and reexisted near the beacon from which he'd taken the tape reading twelve hours previously. He activated the optics and detections instruments and read the straight-line route toward New Earth as far as his instruments could penetrate. Emptiness.

Parsecs of space lay ahead between NE794 and NE793. The search pattern would be tedious, tiring. He started it. A short leap, just to the point where the *47*'s detection instruments could read backward and forward and, in a large number of short, jerky blinks, search every mile, every inch, every light-year of the long, long parsecs of that long, long jump out near the rim of the galaxy.

He put the computer to work to figure out how long it would take, and his heart sank when he had the answer. He didn't communicate his doubt to Jan.

The generator was building charge constantly now, and it was possible to make jumps within seconds of emerging, giving the instruments only time to search the cold emptiness before pushing the button. When the generator was drained completely by the multiple small jumps, a longer period of waiting was necessary.

Lord, Lord, he thought, if we can find her.

If he found her and locked onto her and took her back to New Earth with the crew dead or alive, oh, Lord. The way she was built, the way she was equipped, she had cost billions. Even after the owners of the *47* took the lion's share of the salvage percentage there'd be, hell, millions. There'd be enough to make Mr. and Mrs. Peter Jaynes very, very wealthy.

It made him feel queasy in the stomach to think of the *Rimfire*'s crew being dead. He dreamed a dream as the long hours went by and he snatched sleep while the generator was building charge. He'd see a blip on the instruments and take a visual and blink up beside the huge, sleek, beautiful ship. She'd be lying dead in space, but everyone on her would be alive, praying and waiting for a good old Mule to come blinking up beside her.

He'd shoot a cable over and it would plunk against the big, sleek ship and attach and he'd use the cable to communicate, since *Rimfire* had no power.

"Captain," he'd say, "you look lonely."

"Glad to see you, sir," the captain of the *Rimfire* would say. "You've made excellent time in finding us."

"My pleasure," he'd say. And then the biggie. Then the question every tug skipper dreams of asking.

"Captain," he'd say, "do you agree to a Lloyd's contract?"

"Well, sir," the *Rimfire*'s captain would say, having no other choice, "I do agree to a Lloyd's contract."

The phrasing, Pete thought, might not be historic, but the effect was. He wasn't sure the company that gave its name to the salvage agreement still existed, for the tradition went far, far back into the history of old Earth, long before the age of space, when transport and cargo moved on Earth's oceans and seagoing tugs searched out ships in trouble. Then, as now, maritime law outlined the procedure. If a vessel could not proceed to the nearest port under its own power and was assisted by another vessel, a certain percentage of the value of ship and cargo would be paid to the rescuing vessel by the victim's insurance company. It was only necessary to confirm in advance with the skipper of the vessel in trouble that he was giving his ship over to the rescue vessel.

That old Earth insurance company was Lloyd's of London. Thus the phrase, "Captain, do you agree to a Lloyd's contract?"

In any area occupied by the United Planets, the insuring company, to Pete's knowledge, had never been named Lloyd's of London, or even Lloyd's of Selbelle IV or something, but the phrase was still the same, and recognized as a legal agreement in space courts.

And he was going to be asking that question of an Academy hotshot, the pride of the service. "Captain, do you agree to a Lloyd's contract?"

Through the hours, through the emptiness, the *Stranden 47* blinked, searched, built power, and blinked again. Pete explained to Jan that they might be at it for days, and trained her carefully to read the detection instruments. For the first time since they were married they slept at different times. Jan protested when Pete said they'd work shifts of eight hours for Pete, four for Jan.

"Be a good girl," he said with a tired grin, "and I'll buy you a Tigian art generator."

"Sure," she said. The Tigian machine, which was used to create permanent three-dimensional scenes, cost hundreds of thousands.

"And a few Martian emeralds." Pete grinned.

"The strain, sir, is getting to you," Jan said.

He started to tell her how much it would be worth to them when they found *Rimfire*, but reconsidered at the last moment. Others would be searching. To build up her hopes and then have them dashed would be cruel.

But he could dream. He did a lot of it as the ship blinked in and out and the instruments gave the same readings: nothing.

2

Captain Dean J. Richards, United Planets Space Service, commanding the United Planets Ship *Rimfire*, took his ship slowly away from the New Earth mooring base confidently. He'd commanded the ship during her trials. He could feel the life of her all around him. She was a technological triumph, the crowning achievement of a millennium in space. She was his.

Richards would have liked nothing better than to take *Rimfire* immediately into the first phase of her mission, which was mind-bogglingly simple. All that was expected of *Rimfire* was to circumnavigate the galaxy.

First, however, she had to chart a route to the periphery, moving out along the established New Earth range to blink beacon NE 795, then onto the outward range which dead-ended at a small mining planet about six parsecs from the last outpost of stars on the edge of the great intergalactic emptiness.

Richards was proud to be the first to look outward.

For hundreds of years man had been looking inward toward the galactic core. The theory was that habitable planets would be in greater numbers where the starfields were dense, crowded, where worlds basked or burned in the light of multiple suns. There in the heavy radiation fields life-zone planets had proved to be rare, and so over the past hundred years the search had turned outward.

It made sense to Richards. After all, old Earth and the original United Planets were not core planets, but were located in a thinly starred area out toward the periphery.

Richards' formative years as a junior officer had been spent in the dense starfields toward the core. On his first command he'd gained permission to head outward, and he had, to his credit, a sweet little life-zone planet, parsecs from the nearest U.P. planet, livable, a paradise to accept a few of the billions of people whose growth was the United Planets' greatest challenge.

On the same trip which had produced a life-zone planet, Richards had charted three others, rich in metals. For some reason the outer stars produced planets and asteroids richer in those heavy metals, such as gold, which were still demanded by man's technology.

Richards longed to forget the continuing tests of *Rimfire*'s complicated systems and shoot for the rim. In space travel it was not distance which offered the prime challenge, at least not directly. The distance which could be covered in one blink, one jump into subspace by use of old Billy Bob Blink's generator, was in theory infinite. In practicality, the length of a blink was limited by known coordinates. There was one simple reason for the problem. A ship could not blink through a solid object, such as a star or a planet. The gravitational field of an object as large as a star or a planet extended into that unknown subspace where a ship existed during the timeless moment of a blink.

Thus arose the best-known contradiction of space travel. Man had the ability and the power to leap across the universe, but the catch was that someone had to go first, at sublight speeds, to establish a safe exit area, a place to emerge from a blink at a particular point in space.

For a thousand years ships had been inching their way through the galaxy, exploring unknown territory with blinks limited to the detection ability of optics and other detection equipment, leaving behind them an ever-growing network of blink beacons. A ship traveling one of the marked blink routes had only to punch in the coordinates of a known blink beacon to be there. To lay a blink route, an X&A ship had to creep along at sublight speed with short blinks.

Some five hundred years in the past an impetuous X&A captain had decided that he would speed up the laying of a blink route. He got away with one, then two unsurveyed blinks. His third unsurveyed blink merged the ship with an iron-and-stone asteroid. Those who saw it said that it was a regular work of art, a sculpture to rival the best of the Tigian masters. The unexplained forces of the blink had changed the molecular structure of both ship and asteroid, blending the whole into a uniform smoothness of mixed metal and stone. The stern and bow of the X&A ship protruded tastefully from the mass of the asteroid.

Captain Dean Richards was not an impulsive man. He had nothing to prove. His record was the best, and he'd been selected over a thousand other men, many with more seniority, to command the *Rimfire*. A circumnavigation of the galaxy wouldn't change the universe, but it would, Richards suspected, rate at least a footnote in the history books.

On the initial blinks outward from New Earth, the *Rimfire*'s crew tested detection and navigation equipment. *Rimfire* had already undergone extensive testing, first by X&A Development crews, then by her permanent crew, but she was being tested further as he moved her away from the base, headed for the periphery to turn left and use *Rimfire*'s new, far-reaching detection capability to make enormous, parsec-consuming blinks in the emptiness outside the body of the galaxy. It seemed almost ironic that by traveling the unthinkable distances around the outskirts of the galaxy a ship, once *Rimfire* had put out beacons, could reach the far side of the galaxy, and many points near the rim, in less time than it took to travel the much shorter direct routes.

Richards liked to be in the power room while the generator was building charge. He made it a point to inspect all of the probe equipment. He personally tested the weapons. He sampled the food in the crew's mess. He looked over the medical and scientific facilities.

Rimfire was built to spend indefinite periods in space. She was totally self-sustaining. She reclaimed every molecule of oxygen and water. She recycled all biological matter. She grew her own food. In an emergency, she could synthesize carbohydrate edibles and unbind oxygen from solid rock. She was quite a ship, and she was huge, and expensive, and Dean Richards knew that she was all his.

As *Rimfire* leaped outward, Richards gradually built the generator charge to three-quarters capacity. The generator was somewhat of an innovation in that it was bigger and more powerful than any other generator ever built. Since a blink generator had no moving parts, it seemed that it would last forever. In actuality, the sheer stress of holding so much power seemed to induce a kind of fatigue in certain electronic elements, requiring frequent replacement of entire segments of the generator's complicated circuitry. Stress damage was more severe on generators which always had to be charged to full power. So *Rimfire*'s generator was a monster, and had the capability of moving the ship on any length of blink at 50 percent power and up.

In tests *Rimfire* had been leaped eleven times with the generator at full charge. There'd been no abnormalities. Richards didn't envision a time when it would be necessary to use full generator power, but he believed in knowing all there was to know about a system upon which his life depended. The galaxy was big, and they were going all the way around, with possible sidetrips to points of interest along the rim. He ordered full charge and drained it with a movement of his finger and felt his insides slide. They seemed to move out of his body through his navel and dangle there for an eternity.

"Sir," said a rating at the control panel, "I don't know what that was, but—"

The ship was back in normal space. The blink had lasted for a thousand years and less than an instant.

"Systems check," Richards ordered.

Machines, computers, men, women, all began to check *Rimfire*'s vital signs. "Normal, normal, normal," came the reports.

Meanwhile, the generator was doing its magic act, pulling energy, that eerie combination of gravitational and radiation forces, from the nearest stars. Richards let it build to full power. He went over all reports carefully, one at a time as they were flashed on his screen. "Normal, hell," he muttered.

He went back to the test reports. Not once during the eleven blinks at full power had there been any reported abnormality. There was no mention of a rather disturbing feeling that one's organs and tubings had exited through the navel and hung around outside the body. He called in his brain trust, his senior officers, three of them.

Rimfire was a huge ship. She had to be to house all of the equipment she carried, plus the monster generator. She was, however, sparse on crew. A total of thirty people were aboard. Each individual was a specialist in his field. Each had overcome severe competition to be selected to serve on X&A's newest hotshot vessel.

Pat and Paul Victor arrived in the captain's cabin first, then came Evan Waters. Pat, officer and ship's doctor, looked at Richards questioningly.

"Did you call us for the reason I think you called us?" Pat asked.

"If you think I called you for the reason I called you, you're right," Dean said, deadpan.

Pat Victor was a big, bawdy-looking woman, and Richards liked her. He liked her husband, Paul, too. Paul Victor knew more about the insides and outsides of a blink generator than any man since Billy Bob Blink.

"What happened?" Evan Waters asked. He was second in command. The service was his life. He was a good officer, an all-around officer capable of command. He had dark good looks, and a flair for the dramatic word.

"I assume, then, that you all felt something unusual," Richards said.

Pat Victor said, "I felt as if I were having a baby without pain and that all my guts came out with it."

"Don't you just love that doctor talk?" Paul asked.

"You, Evan?" Richards asked.

"I don't know how it feels to have a baby," Evan said. "I felt something. My stomach seemed to sink down into a mass and slide and twist around."

"Mine was something like that," Paul Victor said. "I was in the power room. I checked instruments while it was going on. Then I checked the tape. There was nothing abnormal."

The door opened and a control-room rating looked in. She had a tray in her hands. "Coffee?"

"Fine," Richards said.

"I felt this peculiar feeling in my knees," the rating said.

"Thank you," Richards said, taking coffee. He'd have to speak to that young lady. He'd tell her to knock first, and speak, during an officer's conference, only when asked to do so.

"Paul," Richards said, "any opinions? We all know that we were on full power when we made that leap."

Paul mused for a moment. "I don't have to tell

you that there's a lot we don't really understand about what goes on during a blink. As far as we know, the amount of power used during a blink is determined only by the requirement of activation of the generator. We know how much power it takes to activate, based on generator size, not ship size. If there isn't enough power the thing won't work. It's as simple as that. The same process of activation occurs when there is an oversupply of power. There's some question about what happens to the surplus power."

"I love that engineering talk," Pat said. "All those technical terms."

"I'm considering a portion of my audience," Paul said, grinning at his wife. "Let me put it this way. Here's what I'm getting at. All the work is done, all the energy expended, at the moment of activation. It is the opinion of most that no energy is being expended as the ship actually travels through subspace. Therefore, in theory, using an oversupply of power should have no effect at all on the ship after activation of the generator. Apparently, the surplus energy is just expended back into space."

"Thank you, Paul," Richards said.

"There's a blink leg out past Dyneb where you go just within the outer fringe of the gravitational influence of a blue giant," First Officer Evan Waters said. "There's a particular little tug you feel when you make that leap."

"That's worth checking," Richards said. "Perhaps it's a peculiarity of this particular leg."

Evan moved to the computer console and began to print instructions. The others looked at the well-tailored back of his uniform jacket, and at each other. Evan had the results within a minute.

"There's not much travel out here," he said, "but the Central Data Bank has no record of anything peculiar going on in this sector."

"How about an asteroid drifting into the lane?" Pat asked.

There just were not many objects of significant size drifting free in deep space. Richards shook his head. To check for a relatively small object along the line of the last blink would be the work of months. He pushed a button on the communicator and asked for a report on generator charge.

"We're at full power again," he said.

"Gulp," Pat said.

They stood in control as the captain checked instruments. The rating who had brought coffee without knocking was at the console.

"Are you locked onto the next beacon, Miss Rainbow?" Richards asked.

"Yes, sir."

"Then drain her, Miss Rainbow," Richards said, bracing himself mentally.

It was there again, that sliding of his intestines, and it went on for another eternity until it stopped.

"Definitely not peculiar to one blink leg," Paul Victor said.

"Okay," Richards said. "We want to know why, of course."

After the next few blinks it didn't seem so bad. That funny feeling inside, that feeling that the blink was going to last forever, became a part of them. When the generator was backed off to 80 percent or less the blink was normal, with the same old familiar feeling which some of them had experienced thousands of times. But above 80 percent, wow.

And still there were no abnormalities, no clues, no nothing but that feeling that time had stopped.

The *Rimfire* was moving farther and farther away from the traveled blink routes, leaping light-years at a time toward the rim of the galaxy where the stars were scattered and the blinks long. They rested, and allowed the generator to rebuild charge, within visual and audio contact of a bluntly built Fleet Class tug. They exchanged conversation with the lonely crew of the tug, four of them. The tug's crew had been on post for over two years and were looking forward to R&R on Tigian.

"Captain," Paul Victor said, "all we have to do is cut power back to 80 percent or less. Even when we use just 80 percent we're draining more power than has ever been used before, about twice the power of a Mule's generator. Let's face it. It's just something that goes with the territory. It'll keep the desk pounders back at base busy for years trying to figure it out. We've got power to burn at 80 percent. We're not sacrificing any safety factor."

Richards mused for a moment, thinking of the distance which would be between them and any possible help once they were in intergalactic space.

"As I see it, Dean," Paul said, "you have two choices. One, you take her back home and let the slide-rule boys go to work. Two, we go on and perform our assigned mission."

There was no possibility in Richards' mind of going back, not unless he discovered that the unexplained feeling during a full-power blink represented a clear danger to the ship.

The two officers were standing in the control room. Julie Rainbow was on duty at the console. She was looking at Richards as he thought, and he caught her eyes, smiled. He'd taken time to explain to her that tech ratings knocked before entering the captain's cabin, and that ratings spoke to officers when spoken to.

Julie Rainbow had the most beautiful, big, brown eyes.

Sometimes Dean Richards felt that Pat and Paul had the only viable solution for staying in the Space Service. That solution was to get married, to another spacer. The service gave married couples favorable consideration for posts together. If the couple had it together together, as Pat and Paul had, it was a fine arrangement.

Neither X&A nor the service deliberately picked crews of approximately 50-50 sexual distribution, at least not according to the official manuals. However, no one questioned it when it turned out that way. Ships stayed in space a long time, and men were men and women were women and old Mother Nature had designed the race to be two and two. If you were the captain, and if you weren't married—

Oh, well, he thought, as Julie Rainbow looked up at him with those big brown eyes. He'd handled similar situations with pretty young female ratings and officers before. A woman had to pass an emotional-stability test to get space duty. There were few weepers on board X&A ships.

He put his mind back on the problem. "Paul, there's nothing between us and the rim except one Mule Class tug. When we pass her and go on out we'll be on our own. Before we get too far past that Mule, I want you to wring this baby out. Every jump full-power and then some. If she's going to break, I want her to break where we can hitch a quick ride home."

Paul nodded. "I want to run a few more tests before we leap again."

Dean Richards was left alone with Julie Rainbow. She smiled and he smiled back. They were, he thought, making them more beautiful these days. She was all woman, with long legs. He decided that the fashion designers who had concocted the new casual uniform, shorts and hosiery for women, had had Julie Rainbow in mind.

"Permission to speak, sir?" Julie asked, with a smile which had the potential to outradiate a small sun.

He nodded.

"You are very impressive when you're being businesslike."

"Thank you," he said, but he was thinking, Well, this one may be a bit more difficult to handle than some of the others.

Nothing broke, but the feeling of vast time and eerie internal sensations was still there when the ship blinked at full power. Richards was about ready to admit that the thing was just the nature of the beast and go on about his mission, using no more than 80 percent power. But there was a fine jump coming up, one of the longer ones of the entire system. It was not just light-years, but parsecs. He'd give the generator one more test at full power on that long blink, and then he'd make his final decision. After the next blink, it would be go or no go. He would either call back and report the strange sensations to the scientists at X&A Headquarters, or he'd head for the emptiness out beyond the periphery.

The blink was made during Julie Rainbow's shift at the control panel. "Full charge, sir," she said.

"Leave us leap, Miss Rainbow," Richards said. The last syllable, "bow," lingered in his ears as time stopped and that eerie feeling in his stomach came to be a part of him forever, and forever, and forever.

He could feel himself moving, could see his extended hand. He knew that his hand was in the process of moving, because his brain had sent the messages for movement. His hand was coming from rest on the arm of his command chair with the intention of brushing back his hair from his forehead. His hand was moving, but it was moving so slowly that he couldn't see the movement. It was moving so slowly that it would take eons for that hand to reach his forehead. His hand would be moving for immeasurable time, lifting, and in that eon Julie Rainbow's hand would be lifting from the switch which had activated the generator.

He knew the feeling of timelessness would end. It had ended before. There was no panic. His mind worked at normal speed, or at what seemed to him to be normal speed, and he could see the instruments and Julie and he couldn't order his hand to stop moving toward his forehead because his brain had ordered the movement and the neural pathways were clogged with that order.

He could feel the impulse, the order, that tiny charge of electrical energy which was journeying from his brain to his hand. He could do nothing to stop the flow of that order. He could not blink his eyes. He tried to move his eyes, and felt the order go out and felt the infinitesimal beginning of movement and in thousands and thousands of years he'd be able to see the clock, on the port side of control.

He realized, then, that it was going to go on and on. He sent the order to his vocal cords and was sad, because he knew that someday, eons away, when the universe as he knew it was altered, when the old Earth and the United Planets had long been consumed by their respective suns, the order would reach his throat and then over the next few eons the words would come thundering out. "My God."

He could think, and that added to the horror, to be aware. He was, for all practical purposes, alone. He could see Julie Rainbow, and there was a vast emptiness in him, for he knew that close as he was to her, he'd never, never be able to kiss those full lips, he would not even be able to communicate with her. He'd be alone forever with that sliding feeling in his guts.

Ships had been lost, but only a few. Space travel was the safest, statistically, of all forms of travel. You were safer on a spaceship than in your living room in a major city on a highly civilized planet. He searched his memory. Yes, ships had disappeared, mostly during the war of a thousand years past.

It gave him something to think about. In the tensions of action had fleet captains built generators to full power needlessly? Were there other ships caught in time and space like *Rimfire*? Were there men and women, thought to be long dead, alive, watching the slow eons crawl past with unblinking eyes, with that sliding, twisting eeriness in their bellies?

He prayed. He prayed for others caught in the same web. He prayed for the crew and for *Rimfire*. He knew that he'd have plenty of time to say all the prayers he could remember and all that he could compose himself.

He thought of the old Bible, that ancient book of odd, strange, and strangely beautiful language, the language of a young race.

"Our father, which art in Heaven, hallowed be thy name."

He would be mad, of course. His active mind was imprisoned inside a frozen body. He could feel and sense the working mechanisms inside him. He would not age. Julie Rainbow would not age. He would be a raving madman inside a timeless prison.

He passed time by exploring his own body. There was a strange freedom for his mind to roam, to feel things he'd never felt before. When he discovered that he could do something which men had tried to do for thousands of years, he knew that he would not go insane for a long time. He could unlock the doors to that vast and little-known portion of his mind, the unconscious, and he knew with certainty that the theorists were right. Men had thought for thousands of years that the unconscious mind recorded every detail of every sensation fed into the brain. For the entire lifetime of man that vast storehouse of sensation, memory, knowledge had offered challenge, and no man had ever discovered how to unlock it completely, but in that frozen continuum Dean Richards went back to beyond birth and experienced the sensations of being in his mother's womb.

The possibilities were endless. He had lived a full life, and each minute sensation was there to be relived. When he finished with that, when he tired of that, there were books, entire books, every word, every page recorded there in his memory.

The Bible alone would offer him entertainment for a few years, because he'd elected to study Old English while in the Academy and had fallen in love with the roll and thunder of it. Then there was Shakespeare.

No, he would not go mad. Not for a long, long time.

3

"Pete," Jan said, "are we having our first fight?"

The *Stranden 47* had been searching the direct line between blink beacons NE794 and NE793 for over seventy-two hours. Jan had watched Pete grow gradually tireder and tireder as he insisted on pulling eight-hour shifts to her four hours. So she simply did not wake him up. She pulled eight hours and then had to shake him hard to awaken him from a deep sleep.

Pete felt amazingly rested. As she walked back to the control room with him he grinned at her and said, "You see, I told you it was just a matter of learning how to sleep fast. I feel as rested after four hours' sleep as I would have after eight."

"That's good, dear," Jan said.

Then he saw the clock and said, "Now why did you go and do that? I told you how it was going to be."

"You needed some rest," she said. "I'm not a baby. I can work eight hours."

"I don't want you working eight hours," he yelled. "I'm the captain of this ship, and when I say wake me in four hours that's exactly what I mean."

And then, "No, dammit, we are not having our first fight. I'm just telling you—" He stopped yelling, grinned at her. She came to him and inserted herself into his arms with a contented little sigh.

"Thanks, honey," he said.

"I miss you," she whispered.

"Me too."

Twice during his eight hours he went to the bedroom just to look at her and to count his blessings.

It was a slow and tedious process. The ship would blink to the limit of its detection equipment's range, Pete would activate the detection units, see quickly that there was nothing within range, not a stray stone, not a ship the size of *Rimfire*, and then he'd blink again and go through the same thing over again. Days of it, weeks of it, months of it lay ahead of him. One lost an appreciation of the vast distances involved in blink travel until one had to cover the same space in diddly-bopping little hops.

During that search of the space between the two beacons Pete got an idea of what life would have been like on an X&A ship assigned to laying down new blink ranges. He told Jan that maybe it was lucky he had a hole in his head so that he wasn't spending his life making short hops, checking detection instruments, waiting for the generator to build.

He made no objection when, on her next watch, Jan pulled eight hours. He awakened naturally after a good, solid seven hours of sleep and came into control with a pot of fresh coffee and some of those excellent sweetmeats from Good Haven, a small planet back in the main body of the U.P. whose soil produced the most fantastic fruits and cereals in the entire known galaxy.

"Hi," he said. "Little taste of something?"

"Ummm," she said, reaching for a sweet. It was deliciously gooey and sticky, and she licked her fingers after eating it. He leaned over and kissed her.

"You taste good," he said.

"You, too. Sweet."

"I'm always sweet. No action?" He punched the computer and got a quick read of the past seven hours. He wasn't checking up on her. She'd demonstrated that she'd learned well. It was just good policy to double-check. She did the same when she relieved him.

"As you see," she said.

"More coffee?"

"You're a doll," she said, holding out her mug.

"Ever consider how little important things change?" he mused. "This stuff. Coffee. It goes back into the dim, distant history of man. Back when there was only good, old Earth and it looked as if the race was intent on destroying itself with endless wars. Guys on duty on watercraft drank this stuff from wooden cups, or whatever they had then. I'll bet it tasted just as good then as it does now."

"My friendly philosopher," Jan said. "Pete—"

He looked up at her, lifting his eyes from the cream-whitened coffee.

"I was playing around with that tape. The one from NE794?"

"Yeah?"

"I want you to hear something," she said. She punched buttons. The brief, ghostly signal came into his ears, and then repeated itself several more times.

"You've stretched it out just slightly," he said. He'd noted the elapsed time on the meter of the communications bank. The original signal, microseconds long, had lasted twice as long.

"No," she said.

"What do you mean, no?"

"I mean it's not stretched. What you're hearing is the entire signal. Remember that little area which we thought might have been just a manufacturer's defect in the coating, or maybe an emission of some sort of energy which the tape was not designed to record? Well, I was fiddling with things. Frequency-distortion correction and things like that."

"Lord, you didn't mess up the original tape," he said.

"No. I used a duplicate to play with."

"So what did you do?"

"I don't know, really. I was just playing with the machine to pass the time while the generator was building charge and I noticed that I could change the characteristic of the sound by making certain adjustments."

He nodded. "Honey, it doesn't mean anything. Actually, the sound we hear on that signal bears no direct relationship to the signal itself. A pre-blink signal is a kind of emission which is unique, and when it was first discovered there were no machines to convert it into something which our senses could detect. It's not sound, of course, nor light, nor anything but what it is. So they just arbitrarily chose to make the signal activate a sound-generating unit so that there'd be some way, other than looking at a sensitive meter, to know that a pre-blink signal was there."

She nibbled at another sweetmeat. "So all I did was just alter the tone of the sound?"

"I'm afraid so."

"But that small area on the tape isn't like a regular blink signal. How did it get transcribed into sound waves?"

He thought about it and it seemed to go around and around in his head. His fingers went up to toy with the dent in his skull over his ear.

Jan was immediately sorry. She hadn't intended to pose a problem which would touch him in what he thought was his weak area.

"Well, never mind," she said. "Look, the generator's been drained. I used all of it in small jumps and now she's building." She wiped her hands on a napkin, licked her lips, lifted herself from her chair to sit on his lap. "We have at least twenty minutes. Can you think of some way to spend it?"

He could. He did. He left her sleeping peacefully and went to the control room. There he checked charge, decided to let the generator continue to build, punched up the tape she'd been playing with. He used the computer to analyze, and there was no difference between the first half of the signal, that ghostly beginning of a pre-blink emission, and the second half, which had been nothing more than a disturbed area on the coating of the tape.

He rubbed his dent and tried to reason it out. He ran the problem through the computer and found that the odds against Jan's hitting the exact tone of that sound, starting with what was, in effect, nothing, were astronomical.

The generator was on full charge. He started

working, making the small leaps until he had the big beast drained down, finding nothing, then it was charge time again and he was back at the console, playing with Jan's tape. He started from the original and began to adjust and tinker with the various sophisticated adjustments which were designed to enhance, refine, delete certain overtones, and he had to get help from the computer to arrive at the same sound Jan had found by accident. But it was there. First of all that disturbed area of tape was converted to a level of sound so low that it had to be amplified thousands of times and then the gadgets began twisting and enhancing and then it was there, not just a ghostly beginning but a good beginning to a pre-blink signal.

He pulled a complete pre-blink signal from the *47*'s permanent tapes and did the same tricks with it. He could alter the tone of it, tune it, at will, once he programmed the process into the computer. But it still meant nothing, for all he was doing was altering the tone of sound. He was not changing the basic pre-blink signal in the slightest, only the by-product of that signal after the unique emission had been converted into audible waves. He shrugged and put the tapes away and concentrated on the search as the hours crawled by slowly.

With two hours to go before he woke Jan he began to think about the tapes again. Pre-blink signals were all the same. There was no such thing as different frequencies. The pre-blink signal had no wavelength. It was different, as different as light from sound. It could not be tuned, or altered, in any way.

Could it?

He shook his head. At least not by an Academy kick-out with a hole in his head.

But there was a thought somewhere, or at least a near thought, which haunted him as he went about the familiar routine of search. He pounded his head with his fist. It was not the first time he had silently cursed his inability to form an elusive thought, to break through the barrier that seemed to block him off from a part of his thinking ability.

"Damn, damn, damn," he muttered.

He was slumped in his chair, fingering the dent in his head, when Jan, fresh from sleep, awake a bit early, came in with the coffee. Her heart went out to him as she saw the look of intensity on his face, saw the fingers moving in a little frenzy of motion over the little depression in his skull.

She occasionally tired of wearing the simple silken singlet. She'd dressed in a frilly little frock which was suitable for nothing much but entertaining at the Spacer's Rest and for making her husband forget any problems. He broke into a wide smile when he saw her, and then the coffee was good, and the talk good. The dress reminded him of the time when he was talking his head off trying to persuade her to marry him, and he was thinking seriously about letting the damned generator sit on full charge for a while. There were sweeter things to do than search endlessly for a ship that might or might not have been blown to nothing.

"I think we deserve a little time off," he grinned at her.

"You're the skipper," she said.

He rose, bent to kiss her. "Race you to the bedroom."

"No fair," she said. "My legs are shorter than yours."

"I'll give you a head start."

"That sounds fair," she said, reaching up to kiss him.

Oh, God, she was beautiful. She deserved all the best things that the galaxy had to offer her, not the isolation of life on board a Mule. She deserved much more than life had handed her, a tour of duty in a whorehouse, a broken-down tugboat loser.

And he had a way to give it to her. All he had to do was find *Rimfire*.

It blazed into his mind like a runaway comet.

"The pre-blink signal guides the ship," he said, straightening suddenly.

"That, sir, is an abrupt change of subject," Jan said.

"Jan, that's what it's for. It has to be. All these centuries we've been looking on it as just something which was there, and we've even looked for ways to get rid of it because in times of war an enemy ship could have advance warning because of it. But it has to be there."

"I'm lost," Jan admitted.

"Don't you see?" He bent over her, his hands on the arms of her chair, his face near hers. "Look, we talk about locking onto the next blink beacon, right? It's standard procedure. An officer says, 'Lock onto blink beacon so-and-so.' But there's nothing to lock onto, because a blink beacon doesn't broadcast a signal or anything. It's just there. It has relay and recording equipment. But we 'lock onto' a beacon by inserting a predetermined coordinate into the navigation computer. We can even pick a coordinate at random and leap out into an area where there's no blink beacon, if we want to risk it."

"I agree," Jan said. "But I don't see where you're going with this."

"We don't know a helluva lot about what goes on when a ship is in subspace." He fingered his skull. "What if subspace is dimensionless and infinite? Some say it is. We dump a ship into it by the power of a generator. That ship has no motion, Jan. It can be sitting absolutely stationary when a blink begins and it's absolutely stationary when the blink ends. And yet there's movement in subspace, movement of some kind. That ship has to know where to go in subspace in order to emerge at a particular point in real space."

"So?" she asked.

"So the pre-blink signal points the way." He was pacing now, his fingers actually scratching at the dent. "Or maybe the pre-blink *is* the ship, and it arrives in the subspace form in the form of the pre-blink and—" He halted. "Damn, damn, damn."

She recognized the symptom. He'd come up against a blank wall in his thinking.

"You're doing pretty good for a guy with a hole in his head," she said encouragingly. "Go on."

"It's silly," he said.

"Not at all. You're making sense."

"Yeah, old Peter Jaynes figures out things that the scientists have been working on for centuries."

"Why not?" she asked. "Billy Bob Blink was a TV repairman."

Lord, she had faith in him, and he was stupid, stupid, unable to think. He paced.

"The basic design of the blink generator hasn't changed in a thousand years," he said. He was just blowing smoke. He knew it. He was just acting as if he could think to earn the admiration of the person who was his life.

"No reason to change it," he said. "You can't improve on the perfect machine."

"But you're saying that it could be changed?" she asked.

"Oh, sure. Well, it has been changed. The first one had just enough power to blink an egg ten feet across Billy Bob's workshop, and it was ten by ten feet itself and tied into a computer the size of this ship. They've made them smaller."

He envisioned a generator. The heart of it was amazingly simple, an electronically shaped magnetic field in a cloud chamber, highly compressed. Most of the bulk of a generator was made up of the computer, which was necessary to make the multibillion calculations required to shape the magnetic charge, and by the ionized chambers in which the charge was stored.

"Pete, maybe you'd better sleep on it," Jan suggested. "You'll have a fresh perspective on whatever it is you're working toward when you're rested."

"There's a body of research," he muttered, speaking to himself. He pounded the thumb end of his fist onto his forehead. Jan could hear the sound of it, *thump, thump, thump*. She cringed, almost rose to stop him, then sighed and sat back.

"Now who the hell was it?" he asked. "Larson. Parson." *Thump, thump.*

"You're going to beat your brains out," she said. "What's left of them?"

He paced. "Person. Lewson." He snapped his fingers. "Geson. Jan, punch up Alex Geson on the library viewer. What I want is something about the field mechanics of a blink generator."

She had it within seconds. "Alex J. Geson," she said. "*A Definitive Study of Blink Field Mechanics.*"

"That's it." He sat and started rolling the film.

To Jan, it was a mishmash of complicated formulae, of incomprehensible scientific jargon. It took Pete back to second-year theory classes at the Academy. He skipped, read, fingered his skull, drank the coffee which Jan poured him. After two hours he was flipping back and forth between an analysis of the field in the first blink generators and what was, at the time of Geson's work, a modern generator. Geson himself was long dead. His book was a standard on the subject of the blink field, and it was over three hundred years old. The work traced the development of the generator from its beginning, and much of the experimentation done by Geson had been termed useless. Endless experimentation had proved that only one configuration of magnetic field produced the blink effect. Only one configuration would cause an object, or a man, to cease to exist and exist almost simultaneously in another spot. Change the field and you had an expensive, powerful magnet capable of doing nothing but moving ions inside the cloud chamber.

But there was something there, something which kept nagging at Pete. He turned off the reader, sighed. "Jan, I know I'm not much, but will you take a gamble with me?"

"Don't you talk about my man like that," she said, rising to go to him, to press against his shoulder and sooth her hand over his rumpled hair. "But I'll take any gamble with you."

"It's just money," he said. "A good chunk out of our pay for this tour."

"You do what you need to do," she said.

He swiveled to the communications panel and activated the Blinkstater. It took a half hour to perform what could have been considered a minor miracle. He was connected to a computer long, long parsecs away on old Earth.

All Academy cadets visited Earth at least once. The plebe class took their first outing on Earth. It would always be a high spot in Pete Jaynes' life. There he'd seen the museums, the preserved city, the vast, hundred-acre tract of original wilderness. The air had been cleaned over the centuries of its pre-space-age pollution. The streams ran clear and sweet. It had been like coming home. No one ever visited old Earth without that feeling, because from that small, blue planet man had struggled up over a thousand years ago, had flexed his wings on flying bombs, on combustion rockets. He'd walked on Earth's satellite in a miracle of dangerous engineering with those old fire-breathing dragons. He'd been crowded in his billions there on the good, blue planet, and he'd come close to possible termination of the race with his nuclear weapons. He'd actually detonated nuclear bombs in the clean, sweet air, oblivious to the poison of radioactivity. And then a TV repairman started fiddling with a compressed magnetic field and sent an egg ten feet across his workshop.

Old Earth.

"I'm going to take you there," he promised Jan, as the Earthside Space Information computer flashed a set fee figure on the screen to cause him to gulp. The price had gone up. Man, had it ever. Well, you couldn't have every ship in space and every computer on the United Planets digging into old Earth's store of information. The computers there, complete as they were, wouldn't stand the traffic.

He punched in his order and waited. The ship's computer accepted the blinked information with blinking lights and a low hum, and then it was over in seconds and he'd spent more money at one time than he'd ever spent in his life. They'd have enough left, after the advances were deducted from their tour pay and bonus, after paying for that few seconds of Earth computer time, to spend maybe one week on Tigian before shipping out again.

He had to find the *Rimfire* now. He just had to. And he was frightened. There he was, a man with a hole in his head, a man who had lost his power of deductive reason, thinking he could discover something that millions of scientists had overlooked.

He gulped coffee and punched buttons.

The information he'd purchased from the museum computer on old Earth came up on the tape, and he fiddled with sound.

First there was a copy of the first recording of a pre-blink signal, taken from the original machine built by Billy Bob Blink. Then, at one-hundred-year intervals, there were the sounds of pre-blink signals taken from ships which represented the state of the generator art at the time.

"Pete, what is it?" Jan asked, when he froze, turned, stared at her with eyes wider than usual.

"Just bear with me, kid," he said. "Maybe I haven't blown our money in vain."

He punched information into the computer, worked for three solid hours, not at all sleepy, and then he sat back and listened, and there were the comparisons. He grinned at Jan in triumph.

"Lock us in on NE793 and leap," he said. "I'll tell you about it when we get there."

Jan obeyed. Before she pushed the blink button she said, "There's a ship between us and 793."

"Yeah," Pete said. "That would be the Fleet Class tug from downrange toward New Earth. It doesn't matter."

He'd been doing some thinking about that Fleet Class tug during the long days of search. She had the same information he had, that *Rimfire* had last been reported at NE793 on the New Earth range. Her crew would be doing exactly what he was doing, taking short blinks, searching the blink lane, coming to meet the *47* somewhere between the two beacons. He had been praying all along that if *Rimfire* had dropped out of subspace, without power, somewhere in that parsecs-long blink she'd be closer to the *47*'s end of the range than to the Fleet Class tug's end. He didn't like the odds. There'd be four men on board the fancy tug, and they'd be working as hard and as fast as they could, with better detection gear, meaning that they could take longer blinks and still search the empty space.

Ships could pass along the same blink route in subspace. It was as if neither ship existed. Well, let the other tug do the drudgery of searching the blink lane. The old Academy kick-out without deductive reasoning had something to try. It might not work, but at the moment it made sense. What he'd determined, without needing deductive reasoning, was so elementary that it would take someone like him to see it. It was too simple for a man with brains to waste time on.

The basic design and function of the blink generator had never changed, but it had been made lighter and smaller with advances in electronics. As the centuries had passed, the generators had been refined to store the charge in smaller chambers, to compress the magnetic field ever denser.

Pete was risking his and Jan's chance at a good future on the sounds he'd heard on the tape from an old Earth museum computer. It scared hell out of him.

"Let's go, honey," he said, and then he was looking visual at the last known point of *Rimfire*'s voyage, NE793 on the New Earth range.

4

"Honey," Pete said, "what I plan to do is against all the rules."

"I won't tell if you won't," Jan said.

"If it goes wrong we'll never get a job in space again."

She thought a moment. "I don't think they'd take you on at the Spacer's Rest." It was a healthy element in their relationship that they could joke about something that once had made both of them uncomfortable, her tour of duty in the spacer's playhouse.

"Is it going to be dangerous, Pete?" she asked, after a moment of silence.

He hesitated before answering. His impulse was to lie to her. On consideration, however, he decided he owed it to her to tell her everything.

"It could be," he said. "I'm going to be doing some things that could probably get my license lifted if the service ever heard about it. I don't think there's any possibility of blowing up the ship. Nothing like that. It's just that I'm going to be doing things that have never been done before."

"I see," she said.

"It's all your fault," he said, with a grin. "You're the one who messed around with the tape and turned that disturbed area into the sound of a pre-blink signal."

"I don't understand."

"Well, it's really simple. So simple that even I thought of it."

She interrupted. "If it's so simple, why haven't others thought of it?"

"Because it's too simple, I guess," he said. "A simple man like me believes there's a reason for everything, you know? I mean, I'm not one of the most pious fellows, as you well know, but I believe that something out there looks after the universe." He shrugged. "You see, a scientist will beat his brains out for a lifetime trying, for example, to find out why the pre-blink signal goes ahead of a ship by microseconds. I'm so simple I just accept it. It's there, and there's a reason why it's there, and maybe God put it there for a reason."

"Ah," she said. "You said something about the pre-blink signal's being a guide for the ship."

"Well, it could be. I don't know. I know this. When I was messing around with the pre-blink signals recorded over the centuries, the ones we paid through the nose for, I matched your signal, the one on the tape from NE794, with a signal from a ship of the line which went out from old Earth almost one thousand years ago."

"But the basic design of the generator has never changed."

"No. I wanted to see the tapes on NE793 before I

talked to you about this idea of mine. That's what I've been doing. Listen to this."

He played the pre-blink signal of *Rimfire*, the one which had been recorded on the tape of the last beacon she'd contacted. To Jan it sounded the same as any pre-blink signal, loud and clear, speaking of the vast power of *Rimfire*'s generator. She shrugged.

"Okay, now I'm tuning it, the way you tuned your brief little signal."

The new sound matched Jan's signal exactly.

"What she was doing, Jan, was sending a split signal. There's no word, yet, for the difference. But one of them, when converted to sound, is different. It has the same sound characteristics as that old ship of the line a thousand years ago. I think maybe it has to do with the fact that *Rimfire*'s generator is the biggest and most powerful one built yet. I don't know how to put it, but maybe all that power created a, well, for lack of a better word, a harmonic."

"I'm listening, but I still don't understand," Jan said.

"Well, just suppose that the ship, in whatever state it exists in subspace, does ride the pathway laid down by the pre-blink signal. Suppose *Rimfire*'s new generator was putting out two pre-blink signals, each one different. The destination of a ship is determined by computer, and the computer places the order inside the generator's computer, as determined by the coordinates punched in. Suppose that harmonic, or whatever that second signal is, overrode the pre-blink signal determined by the chosen coordinates."

"I think I understand," Jan said. "Then she'd go off like on a tangent. She could be anywhere."

"Or nowhere," Pete said. "Or in the core of a sun."

"I take it that you think you can do something to our generator to make it put out a pre-blink signal to match that harmonic on *Rimfire*'s signal?"

"The computer says I can," he said. "It's possible because this old generator on the *47* is such a horse. We can leap with a fraction of a full charge, so I think I can reduce the intensity of the magnetic field in the chamber. It'll be trial and error. When we get a sound-tone match with the harmonic then we'll try sending a stat on that power. If *Rimfire* went off somewhere on that harmonic maybe we can contact her."

"Sounds logical to me," Jan said. "And you're the man who thinks he can't figure things out?" She kissed him.

When he first issued the instructions to the computer a red light flashed and words appeared on the screen.

"Your order not within test specifications," the computer told him.

He punched in instructions to override test specifications. His fingers tended to slip on the keys, because he was nervous, and the perspiration was popping out on his finger pads.

"Unusual action to be recorded," the computer told him.

He punched in a program. Inside the generator the dense, compact magnetic field began to expand. He had begun with the generator on one-quarter of full charge. The ship's servomechanisms hummed, clicked, whined. As the magnetic field became less dense, and expanded, the quarter charge expanded accordingly, almost filling the available charge-storage chambers.

"Well, honey, wanta change your mind and tell me to forget it?"

"You promised me Martian emeralds," Jan said. She sat in her command chair, tense, but trying not to show it.

"Here goes." He punched the button. They lived. Things were normal. There was a slightly different feel to the blink, but they were back in normal space a short distance from the beacon. He checked the sound generated by the pre-blink signal, compared it to the sound he was trying to duplicate.

He hit the exact tone of the *Rimfire*'s harmonic signal on the fifth try. The blink had taken them back to NE793. He double-checked, then swiveled to the communications panel.

"*Rimfire*, this is *Stranden 47*," he sent, using the harmonic, and the ship's instruments saw the Blinkstat message go out, but not toward any of the established blink beacons on the range. The signal left the *47* on an angle pointing out toward the rim, into a sac of empty space, a black, huge hole in the starfields. The instruments looked through the blackness, saw only the intergalactic void beyond.

Twice more he sent the message. Then they waited. If *Rimfire*'s generator had malfunctioned and sent the ship out into that black void, she could be far, far outside the galaxy, so far that she would be lost forever. The direction taken by the Blinkstat led to infinity, with, perhaps, another island universe somewhere out there so far away that the ship's optics could not even detect it.

"Well," he said, after a quarter hour during which there was nothing, "it was a good try."

"That's it?" Jan asked. "That's all we're going to do?"

"That's it," he said.

She keyed the message for transmission one more time, worked with the communications bank, turned the signal detector to full power so that there was a noise of space static on the speakers.

Nothing.

"Wait," Pete said, as she started to turn down the volume. "Send that message one more time."

He leaped to the communications bank, his fingers flying, adjusting, turning, cutting out the space static. Jan sent the stat and heard it come back instantly, faint, distorted. Pete wheeled to check the tape, amplified the tape, enhanced it, ran it through an electronic maze to purify it, strengthen it. It was, when he played it back, *47*'s own message. "*Rimfire,* this is *Stranden 47.*"

"She's out there, Jan," he whispered. "Oh, Lord, she's out there."

"How do you know?"

"That was an echo off a Blinkstat receiver. It couldn't be anything else. Our stat went into *Rimfire*'s receiver."

He worked with the panel. "Look, it works like this." He sent the Blinkstat message downrange toward a distant beacon, the communications equipment still on high volume. The echo which bounced back from the receiving beacon was louder than the weak echo from the black sac of space. "See what I mean? There's only one thing that will bounce back an echo, and that's a stat receiver. There's only one possible stat receiver that could be out there in that empty space, and that's *Rimfire*'s."

He did a little dance. He pranced around the control room and swept Jan from her chair and held her close. "We've got her, honey. We've got her. Martian emeralds? I'll put so many on you you'll have to walk slowly, there'll be so much weight. Hell, we can buy a planet. We can do anything. We'll be free."

She was laughing. She loved seeing him so happy. She kissed him, swiftly, hard, a wet little peck, and he sobered and kissed her hard and held her. Then he pushed her away.

"Let's get with the program," he said.

First he calibrated the distance represented by the returned echo. His face lost its happy grin when he had the results. He couldn't believe the distance involved. A jump of parsecs, two or three, was a long jump. The echo came from over six parsecs away, an impossible distance. And yet it was there, repeated tests showed that it was there, and he had to trust his equipment. He had the computer figure coordinates which would put him within visual of the stat receiver which had sent back the echo, and then he prayed silently.

"Jan, we don't have to do this."

She looked at him seriously. "I think we do."

"If it were just me—"

"You can't get rid of me." She put her arms around him. "What was I without you? What would I be now if you hadn't been so damned persistent? I go where you go, buddy."

He postponed it. He ordered a full meal from food preparation's servomechanisms, and they ate in the little dining room, the lights turned low, a scene from old Earth on the decopanel, a scene of white beaches and blue water and white, flying birds. Then he made love to her, and she began to be frightened, because he was so serious about it, as if it might be the last time.

"You're worried," she said, as they went into the control room.

"A little."

"Don't be. It'll be all right. We'll find the *Rimfire* and bring her back and—"

"That's what we're going to do," he said.

"Want me to do it?" she asked, as his hand hesitated over the blink button.

He had returned the generator to its test-specification condition, the magnetic field compact, the charge full. He had allowed a considerable leeway when he figured the coordinates for the jump.

"Hold it," he said, moving his hand, putting the safety over the blink button.

"Lord," Jan said, "I was all ready for it."

"We owe this much to the company," he said. "We need to tell them what we're going to do."

"They might give us orders not to do it."

He considered. He compromised. He put it all into Blinkstat form, sent it the short distance to the NE 793 beacon with instructions to hold for transmission until further orders or seventy-two hours later, whichever came first. He took the action for a couple of reasons. First, he owed some loyalty to his company. After all, it was the Stranden Corporation which had made it possible for him to be with Jan. Second, if something went wrong they'd know where to look for him and for *Rimfire*.

It was, in the end, Jan who pushed the button. She wanted to. He let her.

The *47* emerged into the total blackness of empty space. The viewports showed nothing, no tiny glint of star, no spread of the galaxy. Pete manipulated the instruments. The mass of the galaxy was behind them. It glowed, a soft, warm-looking light in the blackness. He ran a star search. A few rim stars were within detection distance, lying behind them. And there was something else. Something nearby. His heart leaped. He activated all instruments, and the object was only a short ten-thousand-mile hop away. That was the distance he'd allowed for safety when he'd programmed the blink.

"Ah ha," he said, figuring coordinates. "That's her."

He blinked and his hands trembled with the thought of the riches that would be his as he adjusted the opticals. He pushed the button to activate the search screen, expected to see *Rimfire*, huge, majestic. He saw, instead, a tiny metallic object alone in that deep, black space, and it took only a few tests to find out that it was a blink beacon. He moved the ship closer. It was a beacon unlike any he'd ever seen. The configuration was all wrong, and yet it was there. It had a strange lack of grace about it. It was a studded square. It gleamed in the searchlight of the *47*. He sent out a cable. The contents of the beacon's tape made only a small disturbance on the surface of the *47*'s tape. The same kind of disturbance as that brief little signal Jan had discovered. He tinkered with it, found that it responded to the same frequencies as the thousand-year-old pre-blink signal, and then he was digesting some startling figures.

Just under one thousand years in the past, a fleet had passed the lonely beacon so far out into the darkness beyond the periphery. And then for a thousand years there was nothing until loud and clear, there came a pre-blink signal which was recorded to indicate that the blinking ship had skipped past the beacon, flying through subspace outward toward the total blackness.

Jan looked outward toward emptiness and shivered. Pete fingered his skull.

"She went past," Jan said. "Out there."

He felt a great sadness. There was no way of knowing where the wild harmonic in *Rimfire*'s generator had taken her. She might still be going.

But there was another intriguing question. What was this ancient blink beacon doing out here? And if there was one, was there another, farther out? He put the detecting instruments on full power.

Out there, in total emptiness, in intergalactic space, there was a single star. The star was at a distance which made it undetectable except on the highest radiotelescope amplification.

But with that information came new hope. The presence of the blink beacon indicated that once a great fleet of ships had journeyed outward into the darkness. He sent stats, got an answering echo from another blink beacon near that dim, distant star. Once again the *47* blinked outward toward nothing.

When Pete checked the optics he saw a glowing sun. Difficult to believe that a sun, a sun very much like old Earth's Sol, could have been lost in the vastness of that empty space outside the galaxy, so far from any populated areas that not even man's most powerful instruments could ever detect its presence.

Things were getting interesting.

5

The *Ramco Lady Sandy* had a crew of four, all male. She was a Fleet Class tug, half again as large as one of the old Mules. Her crew's quarters rivaled a Tigian resort hotel in luxury. She had the latest in equipment, including search and detection instruments which, during the race to cover the distance between blink beacons NE794 and 93, gave her a distinct advantage. Her crew knew that. They knew that the *Lady Sandy* could cover roughly two-thirds of the distance before the Mule coming from the other end met them.

Brad Fuller and Jarvis Smith were the senior team of the *Lady Sandy*, with Fuller the designated captain. They'd been in space together for a lot of years. They'd helped take the *Lady Sandy* out of the Argos shipyard when she was gleaming new. They were over two years into their third three-year tour on the *Lady*.

Before *Rimfire*'s disappearance, things had been getting a little sticky on the *Lady*. Brad and Jarvis were breaking in a new team, first tour on a tug, and one of them was getting a little weird. The man was a drinker. His name was Buck King, he was in his late thirties, and he'd consumed his own personal alcohol ration within the first six months. He'd held it well, however, so Fuller simply told him that when his stock was gone, that was it. There was food aplenty, but the company allowed just enough alcoholic spirits to make a man remember, with an occasional after-dinner drink, that such things existed.

Jarvis Smith had caught Buck King trying to break into his personal liquor locker, and there'd been a fight. Fuller and King's partner, Tom Asher, had intervened, but not before the more bulky Smith had pretty well closed one of King's eyes.

And there was almost a year to go.

Brad Fuller couldn't understand how a fine ship like the *Lady Sandy* had gotten stuck with a post on the New Earth range. There wasn't a chance in hell of getting a Lloyd's on that route. Four ships per year had passed them, and that on the ranges crossing the New Earth range. He wondered if he and Jarvis had drawn such a nonprofit post because of that fight Jarvis had started back on Tigian during the last planetside R&R.

"Dammit, man, you've got to quit being such a hothead," Fuller growled at his partner when he finally got Smith separated from Buck King.

"He tried to steal my booze," Jarvis said, still wanting to do damage to Buck King's face. "Stealing a man's booze is the lowest."

The situation had calmed into a wary truce. Asher and King kept to themselves, doors closed when they were off duty in their quarters.

When it became evident that something had happened to the big new X&A ship, Fuller wasted no time. He was already blinking to *Rimfire*'s last reported position when he called up the off-duty crew from sleep for a conference.

"I want you to listen and listen good," he told them, returning Buck King's glower. He laid it out for them. He was in position to begin the search in normal space.

"First guy that goofs off, starts trouble, he answers to me," he told them. "Our end of a Lloyd's on this baby will make it easy living for the rest of our lives. We're gonna find her. We're gonna run this ship service-style. If you've read your contract and the service regulations you know that during times when a ship is in danger the skipper of a tug has service status. In case you don't know what that means, it means this ain't no democracy, gentlemen. It means that I'm the man. It means that if I think someone is jeopardizing the mission I have the right to punish."

He patted the holster which he'd put on. It contained an APSAF. The initials stood for Anti-Personnel Small Arms Fatal. It was called a saffer.

But all of them, even Buck King, got excited thinking about the salvage value of the *U.P.S. Rimfire*. They fell to, working six on, six off in teams, one man ready at the end of a blink to scan the normal space while the other began the charge for the next blink.

Brad Fuller and Jarvis Smith were on duty when the ship's signal bong went off and the reading was a blinking ship coming downrange and passing them.

Fuller delayed the next blink. He knew there was a Stranden Mule out there working its way toward them. Now that Mule had leaped past them back to NE793. Fuller didn't like it. It was SOP to search the area as they were searching it. It was obvious that the Mule had not found *Rimfire*, and he was operating under the same rules. Why had he abandoned the search and leaped back to NE793?

"Maybe he knows something we don't know," Jarvis Smith suggested. Jarvis had grown a full black beard. Brad Fuller sometimes called him the Woolly Bugger.

Fuller knew that there'd been no further information from New Earth. If any message had come up the range the *Lady* would have received it, too. And yet it worried him. He sent a stat, limited it to two beacons.

"*Stranden 47*," he sent, "note you abandon search. Are you in trouble?"

There was no answer.

"He knows something," Jarvis growled. It was the code for *Stranden 47* to answer. A man could get his license lifted for not answering a stat addressed to his ship.

"We're going back," Fuller said, making up his mind suddenly. He could almost taste that contract money. He wasn't about to let some wreck of an old Mule beat him to a fortune. He recorded the *Lady*'s position so that they could blink back to the exact spot and resume the search. Then the *Lady* was at NE793, all alone.

"Maybe their communications went out," Jarvis said, "and they're blinking in for repair."

"They'd be heading down the Tigian range if that was it," Fuller said, scratching the stubble on his chin. "No, something's up. Get a cable onto that beacon and take a read on the tape."

They had the information within minutes. Fuller studied it, handed the readout to Smith. Smith whistled, looked up toward the viewer. They could see the blackness out there. "I don't know, Brad," Smith said. "It sounds crazy as all hell to me, messing around with the generator field."

"I figure a Lloyd's on the *Rimfire* would be worth maybe two million each," Fuller said.

Smith sighed. "I guess we'd better call Asher and that King bastard."

"Reckon so," Fuller agreed.

He briefed Asher and King. "I said this ain't a democracy," he said, "but this is a little different. I guess we'd better take a vote on it."

"Smith," Tom Asher said, "you're the power-room engineer. What do you think will happen if you start fooling around with the field the way Pete Jaynes did?"

"Well," Jarvis said, "we're not doing anything critical. Jaynes tells us exactly how to do it. It must have worked for him."

"We don't know it did," King said.

"We know he's gone," Fuller said. "And we know he's off the range."

"Yeah," King said, "and he could be dead out there." He looked at the viewport and shuddered visibly. There was something just a little spooky about looking into space and not seeing a single point of a star.

"All right," Fuller said. "Jarvis says he can tune the generator to follow the Mule. It makes sense to me to think that Jaynes knows something. I know the guy's reputation. He's a good tugboater. He wouldn't be risking his ship unless he had a pretty good idea the *Rimfire* is out there somewhere. I say that if three of us say go, we go."

"I think it should be unanimous," Tom Asher said.

"Majority," Jarvis growled.

"Okay, okay," Asher said. "I say we give it try."

"That makes three," Fuller said.

"I don't even get to vote?" Buck King asked, leaping to his feet.

"Vote any way you damned well please," Jarvis said.

"I'm in," King said.

"Good for you," Jarvis told him.

It took Jarvis Smith longer to find the correct size of the magnetic field than it had taken Pete Jaynes. Then there was more time spent while they discovered that there was a faint echo from a blink beacon from out in that empty area of space. They arrived at the beacon, read its tapes, saw the passage of a fleet of ships a thousand years in the past, saw the passing signal of a ship, probably *Rimfire*, and saw that the Stranden Mule had been at the beacon. They blinked out into normal space near a Sol-type sun. There was nothing nearby. Fuller immediately began to run a search for a ship, either the Stranden Mule or the *Rimfire* or both.

Tom Asher stood beside his partner near the viewport, looking back toward the edge-on disc of the galaxy. It looked to Asher like an illustration in an astronomy book. It looked damned beautiful.

"Man, that's something," Asher said.

King didn't answer.

"What's the matter?" Asher asked. King put up a hand and wiped his forehead. His hand was shaking.

"It's too far," King said. There was a tremble in

his voice. "It's too far, Tom. We're too far from home. We ain't never gonna get back."

"Don't talk crazy," Asher said. "We're two blinks from the New Earth range, that's all."

"Too far," King said.

In spite of himself, Asher felt a little chill go up his back.

6

One small star had strayed from the fold. One little sun existed all alone, so far from the rim of the galaxy that it would have taken a planet-size radiotelescope to see it. *Stranden 47* was not an exploration ship. She did not have the instrumentation to run an analysis on the star, but a spacer sees a lot of suns, and to Pete's experienced eyes the sun gave some of its secrets. He knew that it was a relatively small sun, and that it fell generally into type G, much like old Sol.

The *47* began to move at sublight speed toward the sun, and although Pete had been awake for twenty-four hours, he was not sleepy. Jan was with him, of course. She operated the detection equipment. It was she who located the blink beacon. The beacon was located one old astronomical unit from the sun. It was identical to the beacon they'd examined back there in space. Its tape was identical, too. This time Pete, whistling to hide his nervous excitement, checked current readings first and found something which stopped his whistle and sent his hopes flying away into the emptiness out beyond the isolated sun.

There was a signal. It was a passing signal, just as there'd been a recent passing signal on the last beacon. If that signal had been left by *Rimfire* the X&A ship had blinked on past the beacon and the lonely sun out into nothingness.

Pete checked and double-checked. The tape recorded the passage of a vast fleet a thousand years ago. Between that passage and the passing signal of the *Rimfire* there was nothing. He sat down, fingers on his scalp. It had all been for nothing. *Rimfire* had not dropped back into normal space.

Jan, meanwhile, had been using the detection instruments. "Hey," she yelled. She'd turned the optical scope outward, searching toward intergalactic space. "Pete! Pete!"

He leaped to her side, made adjustments.

"There," she said.

There was something millions of miles away. He began to move the ship at its maximum sublight speed, a speed which was not inconsiderable. The image on the optics was resolved after a few hours' running.

The sun was not alone. Far away, at a distance which seemed impossible, a small, icy planet circled her.

That was all he needed. An ice planet. But Jan was excited.

He squeezed her. "We'll call it Jan's Sun," he said. "And you can pick a name for the planet."

"Can we name them, really?"

"Maybe. We'll have to check the Galactic Atlas. Someone was out here a thousand years ago. They may be named already."

"Oh, shoot," she said.

He busied himself with the atlas. It was something to do. He started with the area of the New Earth range and zeroed in on the big, black hole and there was nothing.

"You've got yourself a planet," he said.

"I want to see it close up."

What the hell. As they moved toward the planet at sublight speed he searched the surrounding space for *Rimfire*. Then they were orbiting the ball of ice. Their limited instrumentation and their optic instruments showed the planet to be Pluto-size, solid ice, with, perhaps, a metallic core. She was so far from her sun that she swam in eternal darkness. She would become a tiny footnote in the Galactic Atlas.

"Pete," Jan asked, "isn't it unusual for a sun to have just one planet?"

"Unusual," he agreed. "Not unknown."

"But usually where there's one there are others."

"Most of the time."

He, too, had allowed himself one crazy moment of wild hope when the *47* emerged near a sun. Every spaceman dreams of discovering a new planet, a life-zone planet. He'd searched the life zone first thing when the *47* first emerged.

"Honey?"

She lifted her eyes from the optics.

"We've lost," he said.

"We haven't looked much."

"She's not here. She went on past."

There was one more thing to do. He sent random stats off into the blackness, searched for an echo. Nothing.

"We haven't lost. We've found a new sun, a new planet."

"Yeah. We'll get a letter of congratulations from X&A."

"Well, that's more than most people get," she said.

"It's time to go back, honey," he said. "We need to get back to the range and report."

"Can't we stay just for a while?"

"Why? Nothing here. We've seen it all."

"Well, I at least want a good look at my sun," she said.

He humored her. He went to the larder and came back with two drinks, sat moodily, eyes downcast, drinking his while Jan studied the distant sun, and the *47*, having been turned, moved at sublight speed back toward the sun.

"It's beautiful," Jan said.

"If you've seen one sun you've seen them all," Pete said.

"But this is ours."

Big deal, he was thinking, as he mentally kissed goodbye to all his dreams. With the salvage money from *Rimfire* they could have bought their own tug. They could have gone out to one of the new planets and bought thousands of acres of virgin wilderness, built a private empire. Or if they'd chosen to, they could simply have picked a nice planet and lived in luxury and leisure for the rest of their lives. Now it was all gone. He'd spent a good portion of the remaining bonus money to get the information from the old Earth computer. They'd have a few days on Tigian and then they'd be back on a Mule at some remote junction of blink routes.

He grinned. Hell, what was so bad about that?

He leaped up and hugged Jan, laughing. She turned in his arms. "What's so funny?"

"Me," he said. "Stupid me. Here I am with my lower lip hanging because we didn't find *Rimfire*, thinking that all is lost. But, babe, we have each other."

"Yes, we do," she said, kissing him. "And it's all right, Pete. It was a nice dream. But let me tell you this, buster. I've been happier on this damned old tug than I've ever been in my life, and I'm ready to sign on for about two hundred years of duty with you."

His eyes glistened, formed tears.

"Why, Peter Jaynes," she whispered, kissing one of the tears away.

"God, I'm so lucky to have you," he said, his voice choked.

The universe was in his arms, all he ever needed. He could feel sorrow for *Rimfire*'s crew, but not for himself. He was a happy man.

"Take as long as you like to look at your sun," he said.

She went back to the optics. She could see the flares shooting up from the disc of the sun. She was fascinated.

The *47* moved at sublight speed at an angle which would bring her to within one astronomical unit of the sun in passing. Behind them, Jan's ice planet was moving in its solitary orbit in the opposite direction.

The second planet had been on the opposite side of the sun. Even after it cleared the intervening mass of the star, the light of the sun hid it from the optics and from Jan's eyes. Pete had the generator on charge, building for the two blinks back to the

New Earth range. They had taken time out to eat. Jan went back to the optic viewer for one last look at Jan's Star, and when she'd finished looking she made one more, just one more sweep, searching, searching.

Her cry was a near-scream. It made Pete's hair stand on end. He leaped to her side.

She couldn't get the words out. "L—l—l—look," she stammered, pointing.

The planet swam there in space, almost a precise astronomical unit from the sun. The ship's motion past the sun had altered the viewpoint so that the planet was no longer hidden from them by the glare of radiated energy. Even at that distance there was a definite disc shape. Pete punched up the image, enhanced it electronically. The enhancement caused his breath to catch in his throat.

The distant planet, definitely in the sun's life zone, showed the blue-and-white colors of a water world.

Too impatient to wait for sublight speed to get them closer, Pete took readings, found a satellite of the planet, picked a clear area, had the computer figure coordinates, and blinked.

The *47* came into normal space at a distance of a quarter of a million miles from the planet. She was a beautiful sight. They were just out beyond the orbit of the planet's moon. The moon was visible out of the starboard viewer. But it was the planet which held their attention.

One of Pete's favorite decopanel scenes was old Earth viewed from space, a good, blue planet, a planet which screamed life to the eyes. And there, in his optical viewer, was another Earth, Earth-sized, blue-and-white. Water. Out of infinite combinations of distance, sun size, combination of elements, another water world had been formed. The odds against it were astronomical. Yet, there it was. A beautiful, blue planet.

He put the image on maximum magnification and enhancement and they could see the swirl of a weather system, white clouds, the unmistakable blue of an ocean, snow-covered poles.

Jan was beside herself, jumping up and down in her excitement. "Closer," she yelled. "Let's go closer."

Pete turned the optics to the planet's moon. He saw a lifeless, cratered surface. He turned back to the planet. His fingers were toying with the hole in his head. He was remembering that fleet of ships which had passed two blink beacons a thousand years ago. And there were questions.

Why was this sun, this life-zone planet, not listed in the Galactic Atlas? Obviously, men in blink ships had visited her a thousand years ago. How had the knowledge of her become lost?

He felt the ship move. Jan was at the controls, moving the *47* closer to the planet at sublight speed. He kept his eyes on the optics. He used the few instruments he had. His equipment had been designed to spot a ship in space, a ship with lots of metals. The planet gave him a huge metallic reading, of course. She'd have metals at her core and in her crust. He could not even guess, short of going so near that the optics could pick up surface details, if there were people on the planet.

There wasn't a life-zone planet known to the U.P. that was unpopulated. Life-zone planets were so rare that a wave of settlement began immediately when one was discovered. There was something strange about the situation. There'd been ship traffic here a thousand years ago. There could still be people down there. If so, they'd been cut off from civilization for a millennium.

"Jan," he said, "I want you to be ready. Punch in the coordinates of the midpoint blink beacon. If I tell you, hit the button and don't ask questions, okay?"

"Okay," she said.

The sublight flux drive edged the *47* closer. Continents began to be defined on the planet below. They were now inside the moon's orbit. Pete was scanning the planet's surface eagerly, but was still too far away to see detail. The startling tone of the communications gong jerked her head around. It was a weak, incomplete gong. He recognized it immediately. It was the same ghostly almost-gong that had started the whole thing.

Pete leaped to the computer and began punching instructions. He knew what to do this time. The program was already in the computer, so it took just seconds to alter the field of the generator, a few more seconds, as the communications gong began to sound, to see the stat message begin to emerge in print and to hear a metallic voice intoning words which sent Pete into even more frenzied action.

"You are in peril, identify. You are in peril, identify."

Pete punched quickly. "*U.P.S. Stranden 47.*" He sent it. The metallic voice ceased. The communications gong went silent.

"*Stranden 47* requests communication," Pete sent.

The answer was silence.

"Who are you?" Pete sent.

Silence.

He kept trying. There were people down there.

Once again their hopes had been dashed, because the monetary reward for the discovery of a life-zone planet made the salvage money on *Rimfire* seem insignificant. But there were people there and they'd been cut off from the United Planets for a thousand years. That alone was a discovery. That alone kept Pete at the communications board, begging for contact.

"Pete," Jan said, in a strained voice, "you'd better have a look at this."

They had been moving ever closer to the planet. Neither of them had seen the long streaks of fire which arced up from both the northern and southern continents of the planet. But the time Jan looked and adjusted focus the shapes were there, long, sleek, antique. They trailed tails of fire.

"Holy jumping—" Pete was mesmerized. It was like something out of a period piece, a space thriller. He watched the antique rockets reaching up for them, the *Stranden 47* herself helping to close the distance with her forward speed.

He put the instruments on them, and they were metal and something else.

Radiation is every spacer's enemy. Every ship is equipped to detect and measure it. There had not been nuclear reactors onboard spaceships for hundreds of years, but there is radiation in space, fields of it, and some suns give off some of the more deadly varieties, so the *47* could sense the nuclear warheads on the tips of the oncoming missiles.

Pete took one last, fascinated look. No man alive had seen such a sight. Real rockets. Real antiques. Tails of fire and heads of death. Then he leaped for the control panel and, with the lead missiles getting too close for comfort, forgot that he had the generator in the altered mode.

He felt his insides slide. They seemed to come out of his navel and hang there for an eternity. Then the ship was back in normal space near the midpoint blink beacon. He breathed a sign of relief, but it was premature. Jan, at the viewers, gasped.

"Two of them came with us," she said.

He could see them clearly. They came side by side, only hundreds of yards apart, more deadly than he'd imagined. They were equipped with small blink generators. It was absolutely anachronistic, rockets with blink capability. He had to do something fast. If he blinked again he'd emerge into normal space with the two nuclear-tipped rockets in the same relative position on his tail.

His fingers flew. The rockets came closer, closer. They were so near that if they went up the *47* might go with them, or at least be bathed in the radiation of the nuclear explosion. He had it right, selected coordinates at random for a spot a few thousand miles away, but in the mode of the test specifications of the *47*'s generator. He hit the button just as the lead rocket, exploded by proximity, began to blossom into nuclear fire, then he was in the clear and the optics showed no rockets.

Off there, toward the midpoint blink beacon, a new sun flared briefly and then was gone. They'd have to avoid that area. The *47*'s hull was radiation-resistant, but not to the extent of blocking out all of the products of nuclear fission.

"Systems check," he said. He'd blinked the *47* in the altered mode, and he wanted to see he hadn't done any damage. Jan started the check. He took the communications bank.

"They are not very friendly," Jan said.

"I think it's time we went back on station," Pete said. "We'll report in and let the fleet handle that little planet back there."

He was reading tapes, high-speed search. He had to shift back and forth, because he'd made two blinks, one on test-specification mode, the other on the thousand-year-old mode. It was on the old mode that he found the information which made him change his mind about going back on station. The instruments had been searching while he punched in the altered mode and during the time he was on it, back there when the rockets were coming and during the time the signal gong had been sounding because of the warning message from the planet.

But the signal gong had also been ringing because the instruments had spotted a ship. The readings showed it was a ship of some size, recorded its shape. The ship lay dead in space at a distance of about half a million miles from the hostile but beautiful planet. The configuration meant only one thing.

They had found the *Rimfire*. She was stationary. The instruments recorded a total lack of power emanations from her. She was dead in space, helpless. She was too near a planet which shot out nuclear missiles to be safe. Pete had no idea of the penetration of that planet's detection instruments, but if they should spot *Rimfire* out there a half million miles into space and send rockets after her, *Rimfire* would be destroyed.

He didn't want to go back. He'd had enough of being scared out of his skin. But he had no choice.

He obtained *Rimfire*'s coordinates from the instruments, punched in, blinked.

There's a limit even to excitement. He'd known exaltation when he first thought he had the answer and had *Rimfire* within his grasp, even greater excitement thinking about the reward, the share of development, when he felt they'd discovered a new life-zone planet. Now *Rimfire* was clearly visible on his optics and he was closing on her and instead of excitement he felt a gnawing little doubt. He kept his detection instruments pointed toward the distant planet. Even as he closed on *Rimfire* Jan said, "Five of them, Pete."

He took a look. They had cleared the planetglow and were pinpoints of light with tiny tails.

And he'd led them right to *Rimfire*.

His fingers scratched his skull, digging, trying to force his brain to work. First thing he had to do was lead them away from *Rimfire*. There was time, however. He eased the *47* closer. The sleek and beautiful X&A ship was now only a hundred yards off the *47*'s bow. He tried the communicators. Nothing. And it was puzzling, very puzzling, when a Blinkstat seemed to go directly through *Rimfire* with no echo.

He was near enough now to send out a cable. He sent it snaking out, waited for it to connect. The distance was in feet, then inches, and he was forming his words. His voice would go down the cable, go through *Rimfire*'s hull to become audible sound waves inside. He tried to think of something historic to say. The best he could come up with was, "Hello, *Rimfire*, you look as if you could use some help."

And then he'd say, "Captain, do you accept a Lloyd's contract?"

He was forming the words, savoring them, when the cable touched *Rimfire*'s hull.

And kept going.

The cable went through *Rimfire* as if she hadn't been there, reached the limit of its length. He hauled it in, tried once again.

The rockets coming from the unfriendly planet were still there, main engines cut off, streaming silently through space, reaching for them. But there was still time. He circled *Rimfire*, trying to make his mind work.

When *Rimfire* came between them and the sun there was no shadow cast by the ship. Looking at her he could see the sun through her.

The *Rimfire* was a ghost. She lay there, dead in space, three-dimensional, real and yet unreal.

"Like a hologram," Jan said.

Pete didn't understand, and he didn't have time to worry. He had five rockets to worry about. They were still a long way off. He sent the ship at maximum nonblink speed toward them, angling across in front of them. He didn't know whether a nuclear explosion would damage the ghostly *Rimfire*, but he didn't want to take a chance.

The guidance systems of the rockets locked onto the *47*, fire spurted in guidance engines, and the five deadly missiles followed the *47*. When Pete had them well diverted from *Rimfire*, when they were breathing down his tail, he blinked in a normal mode and left them to cruise forever into the blackness of intergalactic space. Then he had a little time to think.

"They detect power emission," he said. "If not, they'd have sent missiles after *Rimfire* before."

To test it, he approached the planet again.

"You are in peril, identify," the metallic voice said.

"We are friends," Pete sent.

"You are in peril, identify."

They came again, arching up from the two continents, and he led that batch, too, off into outer blackness.

At a distance which prevented detection from the planet, Pete halted the *47* and tried to reason it out. The problem was that *Rimfire* was there and yet she wasn't there. The goal was to get *Rimfire* safely away, take her back to U.P. yards. The problems there were multifold. First, each time he approached *Rimfire* the planetside detectors would fire missiles, possibly endangering *Rimfire*. Second, he had no idea how to pull *Rimfire* into reality.

"It has something to do with the blink process," he said, fingering his skull. "Something to do with blinking in that old mode."

"I think you're right in saying that *Rimfire*'s generator developed a harmonic and she followed it in to get here," Jan said.

"Yes. And maybe they wouldn't have known what was happening."

"It's almost as if she's caught between space and subspace somehow," Jan said.

He scratched his skull. "I wonder what would happen if we programmed a jump in normal mode and made the leap in the old mode."

"I'm not sure I want to find out," Jan said. "Not if what happened to *Rimfire* is going to happen to us."

There had to be a way. He thought Jan had touched on the problem. *Rimfire*'s computer had ordered a blink on the standard mode and the harmonic had taken over and *Rimfire* had gone leaping off into dark space, perhaps influenced by a reflection from one of the ancient beacons.

"The program for the jump tells a ship were to come out," he said, the words coming slowly. "But if the order is shunted into another mode—"

He tried to picture it in his mind, that instantaneous exchange of information between elements of the *Rimfire*'s computers.

"We don't know what happens during a blink, but we know that there has to be an order to tell the ship when to come back into normal space. If the order is never received, the order to emerge—"

"She'd be hung up between space and subspace," Jan said.

Pete went to work on the computer. He found a way. He assumed that the blink order was in two parts. The first part activated the generator, sending the ship into subspace. The second part told the generator when to stop, and ordered the ship into normal space at a designated point.

He was able, with a rather ingenious program, even if he did think so himself, to give orders to the computer to separate the blink order into two parts, delaying the second half, the emergence order, for a split second. He leaped the ship and there was that sliding feeling in his stomach and for an eternity he looked at Jan's frozen face and could not move or blink his eyes.

She smiled. "You've done it."

They were back in normal space after the passage of eons.

"My God," he whispered. "They're caught in *that*, Jan."

"We've got to help them," she said.

He still didn't know exactly how. And there was

the planet which sent nuclear-tipped missiles toward any ship approaching under power. First he had to get through to those crazy people down there planetside that he was merely a tugboater on a rescue mission. He didn't want to find a way to pull *Rimfire* back into normal space only to have both ships blown up by a nuclear explosion.

"Well," he said, "let's go talk to our friends down there."

7

The *Stranden 47* orbited Jan's planet. Pete was at the controls. He had worked a program on the computer which required only one instruction to alter the blink mode. He took careful note of the launch points of the nuclear missiles. He was in very close, inside the moon's orbit, near enough for his optics to see distinguishing surface features, forests, lakes, the larger rivers. He was looking for signs of population, for city centers.

It was a beautiful planet. In one hemisphere there were two rather large continents separated by perhaps five hundred miles of ocean. In the opposite hemisphere one huge continent balanced out the surface stress of the planet's crust. The oceans were huge, joined in ice at both poles. In the south polar areas was one large ice island which reflected gleaming sunlight.

He saw no sign of man. He saw only the flash of launch as the missiles began their reach for the *47*.

The missile sites were either too well hidden or too small to be seen on optics at that distance.

The antique but deadly weapons came up from both of the continents in what Pete thought of as the western hemisphere, his mind comparing the two-continent configuration to the western hemisphere of old Earth, and, as the *47* orbited, from the single large continent in the east. He could not count the numbers. They came up in a flock, a firefly hoard of things with glowing tails.

"They're really giving it to us with both barrels," he said, as the missiles converged and pointed toward the tug.

He'd timed the fuel supply of the missiles during earlier attacks. He put the *47* into motion, leading the missiles out toward the blackness of space. They followed dutifully, little spurts of fire marking the firing of course-correction rockets. When the lead missiles got too close he blinked in the old mode, and saw that approximately half of the missiles had blink capability. Then he blinked in the test-configuration mode and checked to be sure that the missiles were continuing their course outward into intergalactic space.

He was getting set to do the same thing again when the communications gong sounded and the signal for voice transmission came. He punched buttons and said, "This is *Stranden 47*."

"*Stranden 47*, this is the *Ramco Lady Sandy*. What the hell is going on here?"

"*Lady Sandy*, what's your position?"

There was a silence, as if the *Lady Sandy* was thinking. Then the human voice said, "*Stranden 47*, we're about a half million miles off the planet toward the blink beacon at one astronomical unit."

"They pulled the information from NE793 and used it to follow us," Pete told Jan, making a wry face. Then, into the transmitter, "*Lady Sandy*, you will soon be under attack by nuclear rockets. Do you read?"

"I read. What the hell is this?"

"I'd advise you," Pete said, "to allow the rockets to home in on you. Then set a sublight course which will direct the rockets away from the galaxy before using the test-specification mode to blink."

Aboard the *Lady Sandy* Jarvis Smith whispered, "He's up to something, Brad."

"You get on the instruments and let me know if anything comes at us from the planet," Fuller said.

Almost immediately Jarvis yelled, "Brad, there's a half-dozen vehicles coming at us."

Fuller examined the instruments, nodded. "He wasn't lying about rockets." He shook his head. "Rockets?"

He led the rockets in a long curving turn. They were getting too close for comfort when he blinked and nothing followed him. Back in normal space he contacted *Stranden 47*.

"Have you located *Rimfire*?" Brad Fuller asked.

"Brad, listen," Jarvis was saying. "Maybe they've got armed ships down there. If they send up ships—"

"Pete Jaynes has been here longer than we have," Fuller said. "If they had ships they'd have sent them after him. I think he's got it figured right. It has something to do with the blink mode. Those rockets didn't follow us on a normal mode. Next time I'll try the altered mode and see if he's lying about that."

Meanwhile, he was waiting for Jaynes' answer to his question, and it took a while in coming.

It took a while because, although Pete had been expecting it, he hadn't decided how to answer it.

"We can't tell him where *Rimfire* is," Jan said.

Pete was thinking with his fingers. He was gradually acquiring information about the planet. First, the computer said that the voice which warned them, "You are in peril, identify," was not human, was formed by the mechanics of a computer. Second, he, too, had wondered why the planet didn't send up ships with weapons. Third, he'd been unable to spot any signs of human habitation down on the planet's surface. Fourth, repeated attempts to open communications with the planet resulted only in that cryptic warning. In short, he was beginning to wonder if there were any people on the planet. If there were, they were all underground, or in very small groups.

What Pete had intended to do, before the arrival of the *Lady Sandy*, was to keep drawing missile fire until, if possible, the missile batteries were exhausted. He'd already led a herd of them off into space. There couldn't be too many more. Rockets had been phased out over a thousand years ago. A thousand years ago no planet would have had infinite resources. The number of rockets had to be limited.

He had discarded immediately the possibility that he and Jan had done what all of the probes and voyages of X&A had failed to do for a thousand years, find alien life. The voice which warned them, even if it was not human, spoke English, the language which had almost caused a nuclear war on old Earth before it was designated the official language of space.

"I repeat, *Stranden 47*, do you know *Rimfire*'s location?"

"No," Pete said. It was not a total lie. He knew where a shadow was, a shadow which looked very much like *Rimfire*. He did not know where the *Rimfire* of solidity was. "*Lady Sandy*, I propose that we cooperate. Do you agree?"

"Cooperate in what?" Brad Fuller asked.

"First, let me say," Pete sent, speaking slowly and clearly, "that I have duly, and in accordance with Space Service regulations, recorded the sighting of a life-zone planet onto our permanent tapes, with confirmed date and hour settings. Should the planet below us turn out to be unoccupied, I have filed claim to it in the name of Peter and Janice Jaynes. Do you read?"

"Loud and clear," Brad Fuller said. He was a little confused. The guy was talking about an unoccupied planet while the bastards down there were shooting nukes at them. However, he wasn't going to underestimate this Pete Jaynes again. Pete had figured out that mess with altering the blink field. Maybe, again, he knew something that the *Lady Sandy*'s crew didn't know.

"What we need to do," Pete said, "is draw off all the missiles that can be thrown at us, until there are no more. Will you cooperate?"

"What's in it for us?" Jarvis Smith growled.

"With what purpose?" Fuller asked.

So there it was. They were right back to *Rimfire*.

"You want us to risk our necks to help you clear a planet which you've claimed, is that it?" Fuller asked.

"*Lady Sandy*," Pete said, speaking slowly and clearly, checking lights to be sure the conversation was going onto the permanent tapes, "it is my opinion that *U.P.S Rimfire* is in the area of the planet. My intentions are this: To clear the hostile weapons from the area so that we may conduct a safe search."

"He knows where she is," Jarvis Smith hissed. "She's around here somewhere. Let's let him play with his missiles while we find her."

Fuller was thinking. He keyed the mike and said, "*Stranden 47*, you've got yourself a planet. I will agree to cooperate with you on one condition, that *Rimfire* is ours. Do you agree?"

"Pete, he has no right to ask that," Jan said. He held up one hand to hush her. His fingers worked on his scalp. He had no idea how long it would take to clear the missiles, or even if he could. They might always hold some in reserve, to come streaking out to catch them when they were hooked onto *Rimfire*. He wasn't sure the plane was theirs. If there were only a few men, if there was only one man down there, it would be classed as an occupied planet.

"*Lady Sandy,*" he said, "no deal. You take your chances. However, if *Rimfire* is near this planet and you lead missiles to her, she could be destroyed."

"He's trying to fake us out," Jarvis Smith said to Fuller.

"We'll be in touch," Fuller said, breaking the broadcast link.

"What are we going to do?" Jarvis Smith asked.

"Find *Rimfire*," Fuller said grimly. "Go wake up Asher and King."

A tug man can sleep through anything. Jarvis had to shake both men hard before they roused, and then they were all in control with Fuller briefing them.

After he'd heard the latest developments, Buck King said, "Fuller, you're talking chicken feed."

"I don't call a couple of million each chicken feed," Fuller said.

"They got a whole planet," Tom Asher said.

"And they've recorded the find on the ship's tapes."

"What if those tapes never got read?" King asked.

Fuller frowned. He'd thought the same thing, himself. "Number one, you're talking murder. If we could find some way, without weapons, to destroy that old Mule, it would be murder."

King spread his hands.

"And," Fuller said, "how do we know he hasn't blinked his claim back?" He'd been thinking about that, too.

Jarvis Smith had been doing some thinking. "If he did, he'd have to use the altered mode, send it through those two beacons we passed. It would be on NE793's tapes in the altered mode."

"Along with instructions how to read it," Fuller said.

"What if we got back in time to destroy the tape?" King asked.

"What if we didn't?" Fuller countered. "It's too risky."

"If we got up close alongside and turned our flux exhaust on him it would mess up his electronics," King said.

"King," Fuller said, "I haven't made up my mind whether I'd kill two people for a planet. I'm not sure. Maybe, if things were just right, I would. But they ain't just right. I don't want to spend the rest of my life in the mines out in the asteroids. No. We're going to take what we can get. We're going to look for *Rimfire*."

Fuller divided the space near the solitary sun into a grid and began the slow search process. At least twice during the next few hours, while the *Stranden 47* orbited the planet, drawing missiles upward to be led out into space, the *Lady Sandy* was within instrument range of the shadowy form of the *Rimfire*. However, Brad Fuller was making his search on test-specification mode.

8

Pete held the *47* in orbit just outside the atmosphere of the planet. For two days, with necessary time out for sleep, he'd been playing chase with nuclear missiles. Each time the number dwindled, and at last the *47* had made two full orbits of the planet without drawing fire.

"The computer says they fired over three thousand," Jan told him.

"What a waste," he said.

"I've been doing some reading," Jan said.

"Good for you." He was tired. He'd been under more strain then he had thought. It seemed safe enough to draw the missiles up, lead them in the right direction, and blink away on test-specification mode, but they were, after all, nuclear weapons, old, mean, scary.

"They used rockets with limited blink capacity in the war against Zede II, almost a thousand years ago," Jan said.

Man's last war. It seemed incredible to think that

with a universe to explore man had ever wasted his life and his resources to kill his fellows. But the ancient history of the race was full of war. Before the space age there'd been constant war on old Earth, and almost a final war. The nuclear weapons were ready and primed on both sides when the government of the old United States made the most significant diplomatic move in man's history and shared the secret of the blink drive with its enemies. After that, for a couple of hundred years, everyone was too busy playing with the new toy, exploring space, claiming new planets in the name of some old Earth government, to fight.

"The history books say that they used the old rockets because there wasn't enough gold to build that many blink generators," Jan said. "It was pretty wasteful. All that gold going up in radioactive cinders."

It was slightly ironic, when you thought about it. The crying need was living room, a vent for old Earth's teeming billions of people, and the first blink space efforts were mining efforts, men going out to find gold on airless planets and asteroids so that more blink generators could be built to send more ships out to search for more gold, but, at last, the supply had met demand and the settlement ships began to blink outward to the life-zone planets discovered during the gold rush.

There were over two hundred populated planets at the time of the last war. Nationalism had been, after all, taken into deep space, and the planets of the Zede II group were, for some reason, low in gold. The planets of the U.P. group, made up, roughly, of settlers from the English-speaking portions of old Earth, had plenty of gold. And so the last war was fought for that yellow metal which had been the reason for much of man's strife on the home planet. A war for planets of gold. A war which saw the destruction of five U.P. worlds before an aroused civilization rose up, reached far down to the bottom of its reserves, and brought fiery death to twelve worlds, six billion people.

It was not something any man could speak of with pride. The winners—there were no losers alive—said it was justified and necessary. After all, it was the Zede II group of worlds which had developed the first planet buster, and had used it. For one last time man met death with overwhelming, devastating, total death, and then it was over and for a thousand years English had been the official language of space.

And it was English which Pete heard as he sent the old *47* streaking fire through the atmosphere, bringing her down to thirty thousand feet at the maximum atmospheric speed.

As he had thought, there were secondary batteries of surface-to-air missiles. They came streaking up on solid-fuel trails of fire to follow the speeding *47* harmlessly off into near space. He had no way of controlling, of leading, those short-range surface missiles. They had enough power to break out of the gravity well, but near space around the planet would be littered with them.

It became more and more apparent to Pete that no living intelligence was behind the array of weapons. The short-range rockets came in salvos, emerging from buried silos at only four points on the three continents. Each of those points, recorded on his visuals, was a fortified emplacement ringed with vacant silos for the huge, spacegoing missiles and for the smaller, short-range missiles.

Pete's stomach was acid after a few hours of playing tag with death which traveled with the speed of exploding combustibles. He took a breath. He tried to raise the *Lady Sandy* on the voice communicator and got no answer. He figured they were off looking for *Rimfire*. Well, it was safe now.

"Maybe we ought to go out and get her," he said to Jan.

"It should be safe now."

It was obvious that the short-range missiles remaining could not threaten *Rimfire* at half a million miles out in space. He decided to make one more sweep through the atmosphere. He sent the *47* blasting down, down, leveled off at twenty thousand feet. He was recording as he flew directly toward a fortified emplacement on the large continent.

"No rockets," Jan said. "We've cleaned them out."

He was busy with the *47*. She wasn't designed to be an atmospheric yacht. She was buffeting and leaping in the disturbed air.

"Looks like concrete and metal," he said, as the fortified equipment came into view. This particular emplacement was in desert country. It squatted low to the rocky, red ground, a dark, shadowy solidity below them, magnified on the viewers to show—

"Good Lord," he yelped, as the dark spots on the side of the fortification nearest them glowed white-hot. He jerked the *47* up, added power although she was beginning to glow with the heat of her passage through air. He felt her rock, bounce, leap.

"Laser cannon," he said.

The *47* was gaining altitude fast when the beam caught her stern and almost sent her tumbling.

Pete regained control and yelled, "Damage check, Jan."

He knew she was hurt. Hell, the *47* wasn't a warship. Why hadn't he done as he should have done, gone on after the *Rimfire*? What had he done?

"Hull damage," Jan said, her voice high and frightened. "We're losing pressure."

She was hurt badly. The flux drive was sputtering, and she was threatening to fall off on her side and start tumbling. His fingers flew over the keys as he punched in blink coordinates for the nearest blink beacon. The airtight hatches would close automatically. Once he was safely out in space he could see about the damage, maybe repair it, at least send out a Mayday to the *Lady Sandy*. He'd really blown it this time.

He punched the button and the *47* kept on straining.

"Jan, quick, systems check on the generator."

Her hands were shaking as she punched buttons and then, "Electrical outage, Pete. Generator controls are not functional."

The *47* strained and grunted on the damaged flux drive, and she was losing altitude. Her speed had carried her out of range of the laser cannon on the fortification, but she was going down. They were losing air fast, and one of the airtight hatches was jammed near the generator room.

"Honey, we're going to have to land," he said, even as he felt the ship begin to lose altitude.

He had to fight her down, using all the skill he had. He hadn't flown manual in atmosphere since cadet days, and he was sweating, his stomach churning, as the red sand of the desert came up to meet them at a frightening speed. He read the flux power gauge. It was falling. He let the *47* continue to go down fast, then, at the last moment, gave the flux drive all the power it had left, and the *47* settled, in clouds of blown sand, to make a landing which Jan couldn't even feel.

The *47*'s air testers reported Earth standard minus a few tiny points. The air out there was good, breathable. But Pete wasn't ready to go outside. He killed the flux and grabbed an instrument-tool kit and opened the hatch going back to the power room.

She'd been hit aft of the generator, thank God. The hull had a hole about two feet in diameter. The generator was intact. The reason for the lack of response to Pete's blink order was evident—the main control cable housing had been burned by the laser beam which had holed the hull.

Now and then a stray rock holed a ship. Each ship had some hull-patching material on board. The hole could be fixed. He examined the control cable. The cable's housing was burned through, and half a dozen wires had been charred. Insulation had been burned off three or four.

The air coming in through the hull was sweet, fresh. They were breathing it. There was a slight risk of some airborne germ or virus, but it was only slight. Man seemed to carry his own germs with him to new planets, not find new germs waiting for him.

"How bad is it?" Jan asked.

"Bad enough, but I think I can fix it in a couple of days."

He led her back into the control room, and hit the communicator. "*Lady Sandy, Lady Sandy,*" he said. "This is a Mayday. Come in, *Lady Sandy.*" When he received no answer to his voice communications signal, he sent Blinkstat Maydays vectoring out to cover the area of space visible from their location. There was no answer.

"They must be on the opposite side of the planet," he said. "I want you to keep sending, Jan, while I go to work. It'll take me a couple of days by myself. If we had *Lady Sandy*'s help we'd be flying again in less than half the time."

He was welding the first seal on the hull patch when Jan called him on the ship's internal communications. "You'd better come up here, Pete."

A small cloud of dust was moving toward them. It came from the direction of the fortification. Pete turned the ship's visuals on it, and it leaped into the screen. It was a tracked, armored vehicle, and it was moving toward them at almost fifty miles per hour.

Pete turned off the visuals, his fingers going crazy on his skull. It seemed to Jan that he made a quick decision, for he ran to the captain's safe, twirled the combination dial, and reached in. His hand came out filled with a weapon.

"I think we'd better get off the ship," he said.

The APSAF which he held in his hand would be, against an armored vehicle, about as effective as throwing rocks.

He took Jan's hand, and they ran, keeping the ship between them and the approaching vehicle, to an outcrop of rock about fifty yards away. They did not have long to wait. The sound of an internal-combustion engine, the squeaking of unoiled treads, came clearly to them, and the dust cloud rose high from just beyond the *47*.

Pete held his breath. He expected the vehicle to open fire, expected to see the *47* either fly apart or start melting in the blaze of a laser cannon. Instead, he saw the rusted, pockmarked nose of the armored vehicle coming slowly around the *47*'s stern.

There was a look of extreme age about the armored vehicle. As it circled the *47*, twin muzzles swiveled to remain trained on the ship. It repeated the maneuver twice without firing, came around the stern for the third time, weapons swiveling. And then it stopped. The grunting, popping internal-combustion engine coughed, and was still. The squeaking of the treads ceased. The dust settled. The muzzles of the weapons did not move.

The vehicle was between them and the *47*. It sat there with its rusty, pockmarked armor, silent, deadly. The sun was hot in the desert. Pete estimated a temperature of at least 110 degrees. They couldn't stay there forever. The armored vehicle could. It had been around for a thousand years.

Pete risked a movement, and nothing happened. He picked up a small rock and threw it off to one side. It hit other rocks and bounced. The vehicle did not move. He threw another rock, this time to bounce off the vehicle's top. Nothing.

"Stay here," he whispered. "If anything happens, just lie low."

He left the rocks in a crouch, ready to dive for cover if the weapons swiveled toward him. The armored vehicle was lifeless. He yelled. He threw rocks. Then, with a shrug and a heart which was beating too fast, he walked toward the vehicle. He put his hand on the sun-heated metal. Up close the ravages of a thousand years of weather were evident. He climbed up onto the treads, his hands smarting with the heat. He made his way atop, seized the handle of a hatch, and pulled, He held his breath as he looked inside.

There were two seats, fabric partly rotted, and a control panel which didn't look too complicated.

"It's all right, Jan," he yelled. "I'm going inside to take a look."

Jan stood up, her mouth open as if to yell. He lowered himself into the vehicle. The instruments were labeled in English. There was a tab which read: AUTOCONTROL—MANUAL. He flipped the switch. Nothing happened. He heard a sound, and then Jan's head was peering over the edge of the hatch.

"Come on in," he said. He helped her down. She tried to dust off the seat, and the fabric came apart under her hand. She made a face and sat down.

"How'd you like to fight a war on one of these things?" he asked. She shook her head violently, no.

"Funny things, the old combustion engines," he said. "Used fossil fuel, refined from petroleum oil."

The controls of the armored thing were basic, simple. He toyed with switches. One switch was stuck. He forced it and it went into place with a click. A needle moved on a gauge which said, "AUXILIARY TWO.

"I think it just ran out of fuel," he said.

He pressed the starter button. The old engine coughed into life. "I'll be damned," he said.

"Let's get back to the ship," Jan said.

"Just a minute."

He worked the foot pedals and the mechanical shift. The machine growled into motion, going straight for the *47*, and he turned the steering wheel wildly until it straightened out. "Hey, this might be sort of fun," he said.

He wheeled the machine to face the rock outcrop. There was a red light over a button which he suspected might be the firing button for the weapons. He found a little set of controls which made the muzzles of the weapons move, trained them on a rock, and pushed the button. Twin beams streaked out. The rock disintegrated and melted in the blaze of the laser cannon.

Okay. So it was fun to play with an old machine of war. There might be others on the way, and they might be better-directed. He left the thing pointed away from the *47*, killed the engine, and turned off the ignition switches.

Back on the *47* they still could not raise the *Lady Sandy*. Pete went back to work. He worked through without sleep. It seemed that in the past few days he'd learned how to live without sleep. When the hull was patched, and held, he repressurized the ship and went to work on the control cable. It was a simple job. He had that part of it done in a few hours, and then he was in control to activate and test all systems one by one.

Jan was on watch. One by one the systems were back on line. The generator's field was fine. It was just a matter of time waiting for a charge, and it would be a longer wait than usual because in order to repair the cable Pete had had to drain all charge. It would be three full hours before he had enough juice to blink her up. He didn't want to trust the ailing flux drive. There was nothing to do but wait, and watch.

There were still two hours to go when a new dust cloud appeared off in the direction of the fortification. This time there were two of the armored vehicles, traveling side by side. They were coming at fifty miles an hour, and there was not enough charge in the generator to activate it. Pete turned on the flux. The *47* rose a couple of feet and dropped like a stone, jarring his teeth. The flux drive was completely out. The two oncoming armored vehicles were about half a mile away and coming fast.

He didn't even have time to finger his skull. Wherever they went, they'd go together. It was as simple as that. He was more sure than ever that the planet was unpeopled now, and he wasn't content to let a bunch of computer-directed machines do him out of being rich.

"Come on," he said, grabbing Jan by the hand.

They were in the old war tank when the oncoming vehicles began to circle the *47*. They came at the stern side by side. Pete had been experimenting with laser controls, and he had it down pat. Each of the oncoming vehicles had a laser muzzle aimed at it head-on when Pete pushed the fire button. A wild burst of laser fire came from one tank as it began to melt. A searing blast of heat washed over Pete's vehicle as the *47* blazed and crumpled, and then there was only the sizzle of Pete's weapons as the two armored vehicles puddled into a mass of useless, steaming metal.

Poor old girl. She was a sad sight. Her entire side had been burned, melted. The housing of the blink drive was exposed. She'd never fly again. Jan was weeping silently. They stood on the hot sand and looked at her, and Pete felt like weeping, too. His hands were at his side as he thought. He didn't even think about rubbing his head.

They plundered her. They put as much food and liquids into the old armored vehicle as there was room. Pete drove away from the poor old *47* without looking back. She was useless, flux drive gone, blink drive disabled, all communications melted away in the blast of laser cannon.

He followed the tracks which led back toward the fortified emplacement. He'd seen the extent of that red, sandy desert from the air. He knew that they'd never make it to the more moderate zones south and north of the desert. There was only one place to go.

The treads of the vehicle whined and screeched for oil. The old internal-combustion engine coughed and jerked and snorted. The air conditioner worked sporadically, sending a blast of hot air one minute and a chill breeze the next. Pete held the speed to twenty-five until he had the feel of the thing, then accelerated to fifty.

The vehicle burst up over a sandy dune and Jan let out a yelp. They were less than two hundred yards from the concrete-and-metal face of the fortification.

9

Aboard the *Lady Sandy*, Buck King and Tom Asher were on watch when the *Stranden 47* began to send out her Maydays. At the first voice transmission King looked at Asher and grinned.

"Got himself into trouble."

"Too bad," Asher said. "Guess we'd better call Fuller."

"Why?" King asked.

"Because that Mayday is recorded on the ship's tapes, that's why. Because it's the mines for ignoring a Mayday."

King sulked until all four of the crew were in control. The Mayday signals had switched to stat. The *Lady* received two of them.

"Okay," Fuller said. "Let's go."

The *Lady* went into the planet's atmosphere carefully. Nothing happened. Detection had the *47* located in the middle of a desert, a good distance from the nearest fortification. Fuller turned on the visuals at ninety thousand feet and the *Lady* lowered to see the laser-gun battle, to see one armored vehicle creak off toward the fortification. To see the *47* in ruins.

"They've had it," Buck King said.

"Just hold on," Fuller told him. He was thinking hard. If the crew of the *47* were dead he could complete the job on the ship's tapes, destroy them. Then they'd have a planet. He had come to the same conclusion that Pete had reached, that there was nothing but a bunch of computer-directed machines running around down there.

First, however, he had to be sure the Jaynes couple were dead. He waited until the vehicle had disappeared and lowered the *Lady* carefully, left her, himself, in a suit. He didn't trust the ship's instruments, which said the air was okay. He found the *47* empty. The laser cannon had done a beautiful job on the communications bank. The area where the permanent tapes had been stored was a congealing puddle of cooling metal. There'd be no way anyone would salvage any information out of that.

He took the good news back to the men aboard the *Lady Sandy*. There was just one thing that bothered him. There were no bodies on or around the *Stranden 47*.

"Maybe that thing got them," Jarvis said.

"We have to be sure," Fuller said.

He dictated a report into the permanent tapes, all about how the *Lady* had arrived too late. He filed a claim to the planet in the name of all four crew members. To hell with the *Rimfire*. She was small stuff compared to a life-zone planet. And this one was a beauty. She was all virgin, virgin forests and plains and beautiful, clear lakes and oceans. She was the finest, a real priority planet. Hell, the settlers would fall all over themselves getting out to her.

And all that stood between him and being a very, very wealthy man were a few old machines.

Brad Fuller wished for just one ship-to-ship weapon, just one blaster, even an old laser cannon. But all he had was the saffer.

"You guys know the stakes," he said. His three companions nodded grimly. "You willing to take a few risks?"

"Why not?" King asked. The other two nodded.

"All right," Fuller said. "We know that the fortified emplacements have laser cannon. Apparently Jaynes lured off all their missiles. We got nothing but a tug."

"We can throw rocks at them," King said sarcastically.

Fuller scowled, started to speak, then broke out in a grin. "You know, Buck, if you weren't so stupid, you'd be smart."

He went out over the desert, holding the *Lady Sandy* at a couple of hundred feet until he found what he wanted, a freestanding boulder some thirty feet in diameter. He touched the belly of the *Lady* down onto the rock, adjusted the field, and lifted tons of rock as if it were an integral part of the ship.

"That's just what we're gonna do," he chuckled, as he lifted the *Lady Sandy* for altitude. "We're gonna throw rocks at 'em."

10

When the armored vehicle burst up over a sand dune and the fortified position, with all of the dark, threatening laser cannon ports near the top, was just below on a flatness, Pete cut speed and swiveled the vehicle to turn quickly back behind the dune. Each second he expected to feel the first heat of the blasting, melting power of a laser. When they were safely behind the dune he stopped the vehicle.

He walked on the sun-heated sand and rock to peek over the top of the rise. The concrete-and-metal vastness was silent. Heat waves shimmered from its domed top.

Jan crept up to lie on the hot sand beside him.

"Are you thinking about going in?" she asked.

"I don't know anything else to do." It was a large continent, and a large desert. Hundreds of miles separated them from the nearest green zone. He had no idea how to find water in the desert.

He used hand-held binoculars to examine the fort. He was intrigued by what seemed to be unfinished construction, partially covered by drifted sand. "Jan, I think that either they didn't have time to finish the defenses against land assault or they're covered by sand," he said.

He led Jan back to the rusting old armored vehicle and circled the fort, pausing now and then to study the structure. On what had to be the leeward side of the prevailing winds he could clearly see the strong metal framework of unfinished construction.

It was getting hot. It was midday, and the sun blazed down with an itensity which completely overwhelmed the sporadic air conditioning of the inside of the tank. It didn't take deductive reasoning to understand that their only chance was somehow to get inside the fort. He had to hope that once there they'd find a way of communicating with the *Lady Sandy*, or that he could close down the laser cannon so that the *Lady* could come searching for them out of curiosity if there were no communications gear working.

He explained it to Jan. She listened, although she'd arrived at the same conclusion. She nodded when he finished.

They came in following the outgoing tracks of the three vehicles which had come to the site of the *47*'s emergency landing. The tracks led straight toward the leeward side and ended in an area protected by standing walls. Two other armored vehicles sat in the parking area. Pete was ready with the weapons, but the other tanks did not move.

Up close, the fortification was impressive. A good grade of some steel alloy had been used for the metallic supports and reinforcements. The dry air of the desert had not damaged the metal. It gleamed as if it were years old, not centuries old.

Pete led the way toward the entrance of a tunnel leading away from the parking area. Sand had drifted into the tunnel's mouth, so they had to stoop, but soon the footing was cement. The end of the tunnel was closed by a solid metal door with only one slit breaking its surface. Beside the door was a closed cubicle with glass windows that had been hazed by time.

Pete's fingers went to his skull. Jan was interested in the little cubicle. She heaved on the door to the cubicle, and it came open with a groan of protesting hinges. When she looked inside she went still, then she spoke in a voice full of pity.

"Pete, look."

The arid desert air had preserved the thousand-year-old corpse well. Flesh had shrunk, pulling blackened, brittle, dried skin tightly over the bones. There were shreds of decaying cloth, a military-type belt at the waist, a crumpled, dried holster for the weapon which was still clasped in the dead man's bony fingers. The shattered skull told a story which had been hidden from human eyes for a thousand years.

"That's a projectile weapon," Pete said. He'd seen them in the Academy museum. A charge of explosive powder expelled a metal pellet from the muzzle.

"Why did they do it?" Jan asked in an awed voice. "Why did men kill each other?"

Pete bent, held his breath, although there was no hint of odor from the mummified corpse. His interest had been caught by a metal tab, about two by three inches. A shred of rotted cloth clung to a pin fastener on the back of the tab when he pulled it away. He brushed the dusty remnants of cloth away. There were a design and numbers on the card.

He went to the metal door and inserted the metal tab into the slit, where it fit perfectly and activated ancient machinery. The door began to slide slowly back into the wall, creaked, grumbled, then stopped after opening just wide enough to allow him to push Jan through and follow.

Sunlight streamed down from skylights to show them a large room with various corridors leading away from it. A fine dust arose as they walked. A metal desk was littered with brittle papers. Pete didn't take time to examine it. He choose the largest of the corridors and, Jan's hand in his, walked slowly toward a door at the other end, which opened to them with the use of the metal tab taken from the dead man.

The large room beyond the door had been sleeping quarters. There were about fifty beds lined up along either wall in front of standing wall lockers. On a few of the beds lay the skeletons of long-dead men. There was a staleness to the air which made Jan's head begin to hurt.

They tried other corridors. One led to the power room. The fort had drawn solar power through panels atop, converting it to electricity. The power plant had been built well. Glowing lights indicated that it was still functional.

More exploration revealed more scattered bodies. Some, like the man in the guard shack outside the door, held weapons in their hands.

"It's almost as if they killed themselves," Jan whispered, as they stood in a little officelike room with a desk and file cabinets, looking down on a man with one of the antique pistols in his hand.

Some areas of the fort, unlike the stale, sickening sleeping quarters where most of the dead lay, still had sweet, fresh air, indicating that the ventilation system was still working. Men who could construct machinery to function untended for a thousand years, Pete thought, had one hell of a technology.

He found what he was looking for after an hour's search. The fire center for the fort's weapons was buried deeply at the center of the installation, entered by a series of metal ladders or an elevator which still worked, jerking into motion as Pete pushed the buttons. He didn't trust the elevator. They climbed down, down, and found a room which was closed by one of the solid metal doors, which opened at the insertion of the tab.

Inside, there was fresh air. The room was free of dust, surgically clean. Glowing lights indicated power. Pete began to study the complex panels of instruments and controls. A stack of brittle instruction manuals finally had to be resorted to before, with a grunt of satisfaction, he flipped two switches and there was a low hum and then a click.

"The weapons should be turned off," he said. "Now let's see if the communications system is still working."

He sat down to read. The old, brittle pages sometimes threatened to disintegrate as he turned them. He had found what he wanted when there came a little quiver and the room seemed to move, ever so slightly. He jerked his head up. "What the hell was that?"

He still didn't know all he needed to know about the controls there in that war room deep under the ground below the fort, but he had glanced at the manual for operating the outside viewers. He pressed buttons, praying that those long-dead men had not left behind a self-destruct booby trap.

A view of the outside desert came onto a screen. He caused the topside cameras to swivel. Just a few yards away from the fortification a huge boulder, a mass of tons, had buried itself into the sand. It had landed with an impact powerful enough to cause that little quiver he and Jan had felt.

"Meteorite?" Jan asked.

"No. Plain desert stone." He went back to the books. There was an urgency now. The language was antique, and he thanked God for having exposed himself to a study of the evolving English language while at the Academy. It was slow going.

"All four of the fortified sites are linked," he told Jan. "The central computer is on the southern continent in the other hemisphere. That's all very interesting. All we have to do is get there and turn it off and we disarm the whole series of weapons."

But meanwhile there was a huge desert boulder lying just yards away from the fort, and he was very sure that another would be falling soon. He continued to thumb the stack of manuals in an effort to find the instruction book for the communications system.

The second huge boulder dropped by the *Lady Sandy* struck the armored-vehicle park, demolishing the three vehicles there and sending a shudder through the bedrock underneath the fort.

On board the *Lady*, Brad Fuller cursed. "Just missed," he said. "But I think I've got it right now." He took the *Lady* off to find another rock. It was pretty tricky, trying to figure the exact landing point of an irregularly shaped boulder from sixty thousand feet up, out of the range of cannon. They'd had to waste some time leading off the short-range missiles which the old fort had fired at them.

Pete had the voice communicator working. He tuned it to the frequency used between U.P. ships and began sending. "*Lady Sandy*, this is Pete Jaynes. We're inside the fort that you're dropping rocks on, *Lady Sandy*. We have turned off the fort's weapons. Come in, *Lady Sandy*."

"I read you, Jaynes," Fuller answered.

"*Lady Sandy*," Pete said, "our ship is disabled. It is safe for you to land near the fort."

Fuller looked at his partner, chewing thoughtfully on his lower lip. Jarvis was thinking, too.

"Okay, Jaynes," Fuller sent. "We'll be right down."

Buck King glowered at Tom Asher. "Too bad the machines didn't get them," he said.

Asher rubbed his chin. "Brad, is it smart to go down and pick them up?"

"No way out of it," Fuller said. "Damned if I know how things kept running so long on this planet, but they did. He's got voice communications. He might have or be able to rig blink capacity. I wanta tell you jokers something. Not many people know it." He paused. "When I was a kid I spent three years in the mines out around Arcturus. They say we live in a civilized society, and I guess we do. You spend three years on a mining gang, and you begin to doubt it."

"How'd you get a job on a tug with a record?" Asher asked.

"I was sixteen," Fuller said. "I got sent out by a hanging judge on a frontier planet, a no-good ball of sand and rock not fit for settlers. When I finally got an appeal back to New Earth they brought me out of the mines. Judge there said I'd had a raw deal, that minors should be sent to correctional training for nonviolent crimes, not to the mines. The judge said I'd paid my debt and wiped the slate clean."

"What's the point?" King asked.

"The point is this, meathead," Fuller said. "The mines ain't civilized. Our society is too humane to have direct capital punishment, but by God they've got it indirectly. The average life span in the mines is five years. I was young and strong and some of the older guys took pity on me. But I know what it's like. I know what some of you are thinking, that we can just go down and wipe Jaynes and his wife out and we've got a planet. I'm telling you that we've got to be damned sure he hasn't sent a stat back down the range."

King grinned. "But you're open to suggestion if he hasn't, huh?"

Fuller looked out a viewport. The planet was green and beautiful outside the desert areas. "Let's just see how it stacks up when we get down there. No one makes a move unless I say so, you got it?" He patted his saffer. "As captain of a U.P. tug, enforcing orders or protecting life, I don't face the mines if I burn a couple of jokers. You understand?"

"Let's get on with it," King said.

"Jaynes," Fuller said into the communicator, "how about picking me out a good landing spot?"

Pete and Jan made their way out to the entrance, past the huge boulder which had demolished the three armored vehicles and narrowly missed the entrance to the tunnel. They watched the *Lady Sandy* lower slowly, getting larger and larger to the eye. She landed in a swirl of dust. A hatch opened and a man in a spacesuit peered out. He saw Pete and Jan without helmets, ducked back inside. A few minutes later they began to come out, one at a time, without the suits.

Brad Fuller stuck out his hand. "Nice to see the man behind the voice I've been hearing," he said, with a smile. They shook hands one by one, Jan extending her hand, too.

"What have we got here?" Fuller asked, the formalities over.

"A hard site, missile-launching silos, laser guns," Pete said. "Everything's turned off now. A few very dead people inside."

"No one alive, huh?" Buck King asked.

"I'd say they starved," Pete said. "A few shot themselves. Listen, what we need to do is use your ship to hop around to the other sites and turn off the automatic defenses before one of them discovers one last weapon—"

Buck King looked up at the hot, glaring sky nervously.

Brad Fuller was thinking the situation over carefully. It looked as if there were only six people alive on the planet. Two of them stood in the way of Fuller's being a very wealthy man. He was wondering how he could be sure whether or not Jaynes had communicated with the home worlds via Blinkstat. He wasn't quite ready to ask a direct question.

"Jaynes," Fuller said, "do you think we ought to call in some help? Maybe get a ship of the line out here to take out these fortifications?"

"I thought about that," Pete said. "I could have sent a stat via the altered mode back to NE793, but God only knows when a ship will come out to 793, much less get around to reading the tape."

Buck King looked at his partner with a hidden grin.

"I'd like to look this place over," Jarvis Smith said. "Who wants to come?"

"I'll go," Asher said, nodding toward King.

"All right, but make it quick," Fuller said.

The three men went into the tunnel. The door to the fort had stuck in its half-opened position.

"I don't know whether I want to get involved in messing around with those other strongpoints or not," Fuller said. "Whoever built these places, they were pretty warlike people. We saw what they did to your ship with computer-controlled equipment a thousand years old. No telling what we might run into."

Pete wondered if Fuller had intended giving him the information that Fuller knew Pete's recorded claim to the planet had been destroyed. He had noted that as per regulations, only the captain of the *Lady Sandy* was armed. Pete's own APSAF matched Fuller's weapon. But there were four of them. And the stakes were high. Pete was not a misanthrope, but he wasn't all that blinded by man's inate goodness, either. Men were capable of stealing, of killing if the rewards were worth the risk. However, he couldn't bring himself to believe that a smiling, seemingly capable, old-line tug man would stop at nothing to gain an entire planet.

And there was still *Rimfire*. Pete admitted that his stupidity in making that one last run over the fort had cost him his immediate chance to rescue *Rimfire* from the limbo in which she hung. In retrospect, that last run was probably the most costly mistake he'd made in his life. Fuller and his men had the only available transportation. If, Pete knew, Fuller were as sharp as he looked, he'd have already made his own claim to the planet on the *Lady*'s permanent tapes.

Pete knew that he wasn't in the best of positions. He stood to lose a planet. However, he could rely on the long arm of U.P. justice. No man in his right mind would risk having the fleet looking for him for a crime against space laws. He hoped that Fuller was a wise man. If so, Pete was halfway prepared to offer the other group a deal, up to half the rewards for claiming a planet. Perhaps Fuller would be sensible enough to realize that half of a planet split four ways was preferable to endless court battles and delay.

"We have to be sure that the fortifications have no further weapons," Pete said. "There are thirty people out there on the *Rimfire*. We have to turn off the master computer, and then go get *Rimfire*."

Fuller was instantly alert, although his lazy, relaxed, slumped posture did not change.

"You know where she is?"

"Yes. Within range of the missiles. That's why we had to clear them out."

"You been in communication with them?" Fuller asked.

Pete hesitated just a split second too long before saying, "Yes."

"Okay. I guess we go close down the master computer and then go get her," Fuller said. "Maybe I'd better go inside and take a look here, so I'll have a better idea of what we're up against."

"Pete," Jan said, when they stood alone outside the old fort, "will you think I'm dumb if I say those men scare me?"

He put his arm around her. The desert heat had

caused her to perspire. Her tunic was wet. "It's all right, honey," he said.

"Did you see the way he looked when you said you'd been in communication with the *Rimfire*?"

"What do you mean?"

"Well, dear, you never were a good liar."

"Better than that," he said.

She shook her head. "He knew."

"Let's go in," he said.

He went to a room he'd seen just off the buried war room, a room of files and bookcases. They encountered King and Asher on the way down, exchanged small talk about the size and age of the place. Then Pete was browsing through the books and files. He found the commanding officer's logbook in the drawer of a desk.

He called out highpoints to Jan as he scanned it. The fortifications had been built in the middle days of the war against Zede II. Time of construction, cost, weaponry, personnel, all were duly recorded. Pete, however, was more interested in the later days. He skipped over pages of routine daily reports.

"Listen to this," he said. He read the date first, a day in old Earth's August, just under a thousand years in the past. " 'Fleet away at 0800 this date. Incoming reports state that U.P. Strike Force 88 cleared route junction'—he gives a number here. We'd have to find a chart to know what area he was talking about. He goes on to write that—well, here are his words. 'Cargo consigned to charge of Fleet Admiral Arlen P. Dunking gross weight twenty metric tons aboard two armored cruisers.' "

"What cargo?" Jan asked.

"He doesn't say," Pete said, turning pages. "The fleet left, if I remember my history right, just a few days before the climactic battle. Strike Force 88 caught a big enemy fleet in normal space and destroyed it, then went after the Zede planets."

He scanned pages of routine, day-to-day events in the logbook.

Then he leaned forward, his heart pounding. "I think I know what the cargo was. Listen. He writes that—'shortage of rations forced a halt to the work. Miners quartered inside the fort pending the arrival of supplies.' This was a mining planet."

"I didn't see any signs," Jan said.

"The centuries would have wiped out a lot of it," he said, "and they may have had the mines concealed."

"What would they be mining?"

"What would you guess?" He grinned. "What was in short supply, so short that they had to use obsolete rockets instead of blink-drive weapons?"

"Gold," she said.

"Riiiiight."

He read on. "It got rough," he said. "He writes that men were sick and dying of starvation. Here, he states that he sent several tanks off across the desert, with very little hope of them reaching a food-growing area. All but five of them."

Jan shuddered. "Poor men."

"The writing gets weak, wavery here toward the last. He's desperate. He says that many are already dead. He says that some men are committing suicide rather than suffer the hunger, the slow death."

He was silent.

"Then what?" Jan asked.

" 'I am very weak,' " Pete said. " 'There are only five of us left alive. I had to shoot Sergeant John F.

Market for the heinous crime of cannibalism. Again, there has been no communication from—' "

He looked up. "It ends there. The writing is very weak, a scrawl that trails off."

"And the tanks never made it across the desert," Jan said.

"It would be interesting to know how they found this planet," Pete said. "I can guess. In the heat of combat, with an enemy ship near, ships sometimes took random blinks, risking that rather than a sure death under the enemy's weapons. Maybe a Zede ship was under attack and popped off and ended up here. When they found that the planet had more than the usual amount of gold-yielding ore—"

"This is quite a place," Brad Fuller said, as he entered the room. He looked around. "Find out what and why?" He waved a hand at the books.

"It was a Zede II Group warbase," Pete said. "My guess is that it was sort of a final retreat for some of the Zede brass, in case things went wrong."

"Well, they never made it," Fuller said. "I guess we've seen enough. Hardware is interesting. Computers surprisingly good for the time. I guess we're ready if you folks are."

Pete had made up a quick lie because he remembered Jan's statement that Fuller and his men frightened her. To know that there was gold on Jan's Planet, enough gold to warrant the construction in wartime of some very expensive bases, changed the situation. A war had been fought for gold, and, in reality, nothing much had changed since man killed man and then destroyed entire planets. Gold, more than any other thing, brought out the worst in men.

11

The position of the southern continent was near the southern tropical zone. When the *Lady Sandy* made a test run over the area, only three of the short-range missiles had to be led off into space. Then they were approaching at an altitude calculated to draw harmless fire from the laser cannon. A few feeble flashes told them that at least five of the cannon were still operational. Visual examination showed that subtropical growth had taken over the fortification, almost hiding it from the air.

Many long-range missiles sat in their silos. Vines grew over the launching pads of the short-range weapons, and the climbing, persistent growth had clogged ports of many of the laser cannon. One entire side of the fort was buried under an age-old avalanche of green. After some testing, Fuller brought the *Lady Sandy* down on the bank of a stream which ran nearby, in an area of low, soft growth in what was, apparently, an often-flooded area.

It was about half a mile to the fort. They set out, Fuller assuming the leadership, hacking his way at times through dense growth. It took well over two hours to reach the missile silos. It was, for Jan, an eerie feeling to look down into the pits to see the rounded, rusting nose of a missile and to know that there, within a few feet, was a nuclear weapon.

Armored vehicles were covered with green growth which had sprung up through the paving of a parking lot. The tunnel entrance, similar to the entrance to the fort in the desert of the large, eastern continent, had to be cleared. Once Tom Asher was almost bitten by a reptile which had a deadly look. Pete used his saffer on the snake, watched it become motionless.

This time there was no dead guard in the guardhouse from whom to take an entry tab. The metal door was closed, rusted. The feel of ruin was everywhere, for the subtropical climate had not been as kind to man's creations as the arid atmosphere of the eastern desert.

Asher and King went back to the ship for a cutting torch. While they were gone, Pete scouted the fort, climbing atop it with the aid of the clinging vines which had found root holds in the seemingly impervious cement. He was eager to see what was inside. Around the fort, trees with fruit and nuts abounded. The men in this installation would not have died of starvation. It seemed unlikely that such a variety of fine-looking fruit would all be poisonous to man.

Only the very peak of the fort's dome was free of vegetation. From that vantage point he could look off toward the river. Some trees grew taller than the fort, but he could see that the jungly woodland stretched onward and outward beyond vision, rising into a range of low, forested hills to the north.

King and Asher were cutting through the door when he came back down. They were through within half an hour, cutting a hole large enough to crawl through. Fuller entered first, followed by Jan and then Pete. The large room beyond the door was much the same as in the other fort. There was a desk, but no papers. The dampness of the climate had penetrated, somehow. There were no dead men. There was a coating of some kind of slime on the cement floor which made walking tricky.

Pete led the way down a corridor, assuming that the interior design of this installation was much the same as that of the one in the desert. The rungs of the ladders going downward toward the war room were slick, rusted.

Things were different down below. There was, instead of the war room, a room which, from rotting remains of beds, from rusting metal equipment, had been a sick bay. They saw the first indication of human remains there. He was not well preserved, not preserved at all. There was only a hint of human bones in a damp, moldy pile of dust, but Pete saw the metal of a door-opening tab amid the dust, and retrieved it.

The life in the subtropical fort had been lived underground. There were large rooms with the remains of many beds, food-preparation areas, recreation areas.

It was Jan who discovered the closed hatch which opened to reveal another flight of metal ladders leading to a still-lower level. Pete inserted himself in front of Fuller and went down first. Halfway down he felt a hint of fresh air, cool, refreshing. It carried a slight aroma of decay and rot, but it was much better than the muggy, stale air of the upper levels.

He emerged from the downshaft into a cooled area. As he stepped forward a blaze of light almost blinded him. The room was huge. The floor was fairly clean. The ceiling was high, and studded with lights. And across that room, lying in the open, between two partitions, was a huge stack of rectangular yellow bricks.

"Gawd, look at that," Tom Asher said, having followed Pete down the ladder.

One by one they came down, stepped out of the downshaft, halted, eyes dazzled by enough gold to buy a man anything he ever wanted if he lived to be four hundred years old.

Gold.

Man's history was tinged yellow by it. From the dawn of time the metal had been coveted, fought over, traded, bought, sold, stolen. Countless men had died for gold which would amout to a tiny fraction of the hoard of roughly pressed bricks gleaming under the lights of that room far below the ground level in a thousand-year-old war fortification.

Buck King, breathing hard and fast, started walking swiftly toward the stacks of gold.

"Hey, hold it," Pete yelled. "Don't touch that stuff."

King turned. "I just want to look," he said. He was fully aware that Pete carried a saffer. He was sure, however, that Jaynes wouldn't use it. Not yet. And he had to touch, to feel, to sample the weight of one of those bricks of gleaming gold.

"King," Pete yelled, "don't—"

Pete was moving forward, yelling, even as the arcs of high voltage shot out, lightninglike, from the eyes he'd noticed on the partitions which housed the gold. King bucked and danced, already dead, his body supported in its lifeless state by the force of the voltage which fried him, left a stench of burning flesh in the air as the beams cut off and what was left of Buck King fell wetly to the floor.

"I tried to warn him," Pete said. "Jesus, I tried to warn him."

Tom Asher, his mouth open in surprise, had taken a couple of steps forward.

"God, if he'd only listened," Pete said, his fingers toying with the dent in his skull. Jan went to his side.

"You tried, Pete," she said soothingly.

"We'd better find the computer and turn all this stuff off," Fuller said.

"We can at least get him out of there," Asher said.

"If you wanta reach in there, you go right ahead," Fuller said. "He ain't going nowhere."

Jan stood chewing on one knuckle, her face white. The ventilation system was slowly taking the smell of charred flesh from the air.

The war room was on the lower level. The door would not open to the tab Pete had taken from the pile of human dust. Once again the cutting torch sizzled, and then they were inside. This was a much more complex place than the war room in the desert fort.

"You're the expert," Fuller said to Pete. Pete nodded. He prowled, taking a quick glance at three walls of meters, instruments, controls. Dead lights and red trouble lights told him that parts of the system were decayed.

"There'll be a bunch of manuals somewhere," he

said. "I don't want to start experimenting in here without knowing what I'm doing."

Jan found a closed shelf. The manuals were old, brittle, yellowed, but readable. "This is going to take a while, if you fellows want to go exploring," Pete said.

"You guys go ahead," Fuller said. Jarvis and Asher left the room.

Pete sat on a steel cabinet and began to read.

"This one links all the positions," he said. "We were right in that."

Jan looked at Brad Fuller's expressionless face. She did not like the way he kept looking at Pete when Pete wasn't watching. There was something about the man which set her teeth on edge.

"Don't want him to push the wrong button," Fuller said, grinning at her. "There's still a lot of nuke warheads outside, and maybe some stored inside."

"No," she said. "We don't, and he won't."

"All right," Pete said, after an hour's examination of the various manuals. "Here's one thing I can do right now."

He walked to a control bank, checked and double-checked, then began to flip switches. "This puts the other three forts in a stand-by, or deactivated, stage." What he didn't say was that there in the manual in the master war room were instructions for destroying all of the facilities. Built into each fort were explosive charges which had a series of fail-safes. They could be set off only from this room. The self-destruct stage in the headquarters fort had a delay which could be programmed up to two hours. That one was the biggie. Down underneath the fort, put there by desperate, determined men a thousand years ago, was the most terrible weapon ever invented by man. They were all walking atop, sitting right on top of, a planet buster which would, upon detonation, turn a beautiful planet into molten stone and metal and asteroid-sized chunks.

He spent a few minutes on the section which detailed how to deactivate and dismember the planet buster. That, however, could be done later. There was a possibility, in that climate, that the wiring belowground had long since corroded away, but sooner or later someone, Pete hoped under his own direction, would have to bring that thing up and break it down into harmless components and destroy it piece by piece.

Next he found the bank which shut off all of the central fort's weaponry, and the few remaining laser cannon which were operational went dead as their charges slowly seeped away, power cut off. It was amazing to Pete to think that so much of the fort's weaponry was still in an operational mode.

He went to work on finding the source of power and control for the guard beams in the gold storeroom. It took half an hour. He was ready to deactivate when a frantic shout came in through the hole burned in the war-room door.

It was Jarvis. "Brad, Jaynes, you guys better get out here, and I mean on the double."

Turning off the beam could wait. Pete leaped to his feet. Jan followed him out the hole in the door. As she stuck her head through she saw Tom Asher strike Pete on the skull with a piece of pipe. She heard a sickening thud, realized in an agonized instant that the blow had fallen directly on the weak spot in Pete's head. She started to scream, and was seized by Jarvis Smith.

Asher jerked the saffer from Pete's belt as he fell, crouched, the weapon pointed at Brad Fuller.

"Fuller," Asher said, "you've got about fifteen seconds to decide if you're in or out."

"Tom, you know the two of you together aren't smart enough to bring this off," Brad said. "Now point that weapon some other way before I take it away from you and jam it down your throat."

"He's with us," Jarvis Smith said. "I told you he would be."

"You jerks jumped the gun," Fuller said. "You didn't give Jaynes enough time to deactivate the guard beams on the gold."

Asher looked uncertain. He lowered the saffer. Jan pulled away from Smith and fell to her knees beside Pete. He was breathing deeply and evenly. When she lifted an eyelid his eye was rolled back, showing white.

She was surprised at her reaction. Pete could be hurt badly, having been struck on that area of his skull where the old injury had left a depression, but she was no longer concerned about whether or not the blow had done permanent damage. She was angry. There was a deep faith in her that Pete would survive the blow, but atop that faith was a seething rage at the men who were responsible.

"The way we figure it," Jarvis said, "they can have an accident, Brad."

"That's the way you figured it, huh?" Fuller said. He'd been thinking of some way to tie the death of the Jaynes couple into the destruction of their ship. It had been hit by laser fire. The problem was that a laser burns a human body in a way that no other heat does. If they tried to fake it and a fleet ship investigated, that would be too risky. The dry desert air where the *47* was wrecked would preserve the bodies well.

The guard beams. The high voltage had gotten Buck King.

"Okay," he said, "pick Jaynes up and bring him along, Jarvis. Tom, you bring the woman."

Smith bent over Pete. "He's coming around," he said.

"Okay," Brad said, changing plans. "Bring him back into the war room."

Pete had caught a flicker of movement as he walked out the door. He had seen the upraised arm, the dark object in the hand. From the time of his accident he'd had a deathly fear of being hit on the head. The depressed spot on his skull wasn't actually weaker than the surrounding areas of bone. The doctors had done a fine job of grafting in bone, but there were times when he had nightmares of feeling things impacting on his skull, and he always carried a vivid memory of the months of totally debilitating headaches.

It was that fear of being struck on the head which, in all probability, had saved his life. Just a flicker of movement, an awareness, and he was throwing his feet out from under him to begin to fall flat on his face as the piece of pipe came down and made a thudding impact. The blow was still severe enough to cause him to fall endlessly into blackness.

He became aware of movement. His head was as large as the world, and there was pain which cut through the blackness and jerked his eyes open. He groaned.

He allowed someone to steer him to a metal chair. He tried to see. Jan's face, taut, pale, swam before his eyes. "Jan?"

Jan took his hands in hers, squeezed. "Can you hear me, Pete?"

He moaned with the pain of the sound. "Yes," he said.

"Jaynes," Brad Fuller said, "what we want you to do is turn off the voltage of those guard beams. Do you hear me?"

"I hear you," Pete said, with great effort.

"Move him over to the console," Fuller said.

Pete tried to struggle against the hands on his arms, but a part of him was far away, unable to come back. He slumped into the dust of a decayed cushion. In front of his eyes lights glowed on a tall panel.

"They're going to kill us, Pete," Jan said.

"Shut her up," Fuller ordered.

Pete heard a meaty, slapping sound. He turned. Smith had struck Jan across the mouth. The sound and the look of pained surprise on her face drove the pain far back in his mind and left his head reasonably clear.

"Turn off the power to the beams, Jaynes," Fuller said. He had his saffer pointed at Pete's head.

It didn't take deductive reasoning to understand. A planet, a planet of gold, was the prize. To men like Fuller and the others, two lives would not stand in the way.

He felt a wave of overwhelming sadness. The time aboard the poor old *47* had been the happiest time of his life. Before *Rimfire* went missing and put dreams of wealth into his head he'd been blissfully content just to look forward to years and years of life on a tug with Jan. And now it was all going to end. No wealth. That didn't matter. No Jan.

That's what mattered. Thinking of being dead was not as painful to him as thinking of being deprived of that girl he'd found in a spacer's whorehouse on Tigian.

"Show me which switches to push," Fuller said.

Why should he cooperate? They were going to kill him and kill Jan. He felt a wave of dizziness, almost fell from the chair.

"Quit faking it, Jaynes. Either you show me how to turn off the beam or your wife gets it now," Fuller said.

"All right," he said, holding onto the edge of the console with both hands to steady himself.

Pete Jaynes had never been a fatalist. It was the pain in his head, the dizziness. He couldn't think. He could only grieve over the loss of the woman he loved. And a slow anger fought with the pain in his head, grew into a devastating force. He saw in his mind a sinister thing buried far underground, down into the planet's bedrock. The killer. The planet destroyer. He was too weak. He hurt too much. There were three of them and there was nothing he could do to save Jan. She was going to be killed and he was going to be killed and that was something he couldn't accept without protest.

"Jaynes, you've got five seconds," Fuller said, in a tone of voice which convinced Pete.

"Okay," he said. He took a deep breath. The step he was about to take was a final, irrevocable step. Once activated, there was no stopping the process which would result in Jan's beautiful planet being reduced to space rubble. The makers had obviously reasoned that if the situation was desperate enough to activate the planet buster there would be no need to make a change in plans.

The device was set for a two-hour delay. That was adjustable. Pete decided, first, to shorten the time, then felt that wave of sadness. He left the timer at two hours. He looked at Jan. Silent tears had streaked her cheek. Her lip was starting to swell.

His fingers shook as he lifted the cover of the first protected switch. He pushed it with a solid flick, began to go through the sequence he'd read only once in the manual. He had that kind of mind. He was low on deductive reasoning, so he'd compensated for it by developing his memory. He had been so impressed by the mere fact that men had been so desperate that they could coldly provide for the destruction of a planet that the sequence was burned into his brain.

It took six steps. He had gone through five of them. Lights were blinking. He took a deep breath, took one last look at Jan, and pushed the final button.

There was a sizzling sound from the tall panel. Smoke burst out. There was crackling and popping and then a small explosion which buckled the metal front of the panel. He didn't know if that had been programmed by the builders of the fort, but it had happened. The entire panel which contained the instrumentation for activating the planet buster was dead.

Fuller let out a curse as the panel burned and destroyed itself. He would have to change his plans again. He'd intended only to have Jaynes show him how to turn off the guard beams which protected the gold, then turn them back on. Mr. and Mrs. Pete Jaynes would then have joined Buck King in a charred heap.

"Is the damned thing off?" Jarvis asked.

"Yes," Pete said, praying that it was not. The ventilation system still worked. Other panels in the war room showed ready lights.

Fuller needed time to think, but the gold was blinding him. He could picture it in his mind. He could see it, solid banks of it, stacked over head-high, tons and tons of it. There had to be a safe way of getting rid of the Jayneses, but he could think of that later. Maybe he could simply take them back to the *Stranden 47* and make them start walking. The desert would do the job.

"Let's go see that gold," Tom Asher said. He pushed Jan ahead of him out the door.

Pete tried to leap to his feet. The sudden movement sent blackness into his skull, and he slumped.

"Hold it, Tom," Fuller said.

Asher seized Jan's arm and pulled her to a stop.

"Let's just finish him off," Jarvis said.

"Not here, you dumb bastard," Fuller yelled.

"I don't know about you two," Asher said, "But I'm having a look at that gold."

Fuller rolled his eyes. They had a planet and those idiots were able to think only of a few tons of gold.

"Bring Jaynes," he told Jarvis.

Pete felt himself being lifted. His legs were wobbly, but after a few steps he could walk with Smith's support. He made it as far as the main room where the gleaming gold was stored. The lights still functioned, blazing into glare as they entered the area.

"Man," Jarvis said, letting Pete slump weakly to the floor, "I'm gonna buy me a space yacht and hit every high-class whorehouse in the galaxy."

Tom Asher was moving toward the gold. Pete forced his eyes to focus. Smith, too, was mesmerized by the golden gleam. He took two or three running steps and was side by side with Asher when they walked into the beam and the force of the killing voltage flared, causing the muscles of their bodies to spasm in a wild dance of death.

Brad Fuller let out a surprised yell. And at that moment Jan shoved him with all her might. He'd leaned forward involuntarily as his two companions began to jerk and crackle, as the stench of burning flesh came, once again, to his nostrils. The shove sent him to his knees, and Jan was running for the dark entrance of a corridor as he turned.

Pete used all his reserve strength to throw himself at the bigger man, to put his arm over Fuller's weapon arm. The saffer's charge sparkled against the cement floor. Pete was unconscious again even before Fuller's fist slammed into his chin.

Jan had gained the dimness of the corridor and was running knees high, arms pumping. She felt a surge of hope. Pete, bless him, had tricked them, had taken two more of them, leaving only one.

She reached the ladder shaft and climbed with all her strength, had put one landing behind her when Smith pounded down the corridor. She could hear the clatter of his boots on the rungs of the metal ladder as she climbed.

She'd had no plan when she made her move. She had acted instinctively, taking advantage of the surprise of the death of the two men. Now she had a picture in her mind. The big room where the dust of several men lay amid the rotted ruins of beds.

She reached the door. It had been, thank God, left

open. She skidded as she turned in and ran to the nearest pile of molded, rotting rubble. What she wanted wasn't there. She heard running footsteps in the corridor outside as she scurried from molding pile to molding pile. Then, at last, she saw what she was looking for. One of those ancient projectile weapons lay amid the fragmented bones of a human hand. She seized it.

She knew little about weapons, nothing about antique weapons. She did not know that the pistol was an automatic, that a round was in the chamber, moved there by the automatic action when its owner had, a thousand years past, ended his suffering.

Fuller spotted the door, wheeled into it, came to a skidding stop. The woman stood a few feet away by a moldering pile of bed and human bones, pointing one of the old handguns at him. He had to laugh. It was a brief, throaty chuckle.

"What the hell good do you think that thing is going to do you?" he asked, moving slowly toward Jan.

"We won't know until I pull the trigger, will we?" Jan asked. She was surprised by the calmness in her voice.

"It might blow up in your face," Fuller said, still walking.

"We'll see," Jan said. He was about five paces away. She had the muzzle of the old weapon pointed directly at his face.

She pulled. The trigger did not move. Fuller, seeing the movement of her hand, seeing her eyes go wide, laughed again.

She pulled harder, and Fuller's laugh was driven from him by the impact of a thousand-year-old slug of metal which struck him high on the bridge of the nose.

Jan let the old gun fall to the floor, It struck with a metallic clang. Fuller had been blown backward by the impact of the heavy slug. He fell to lie on his back, his face a study in death, mouth wide in surprise, blood covering his open eyes. Jan screamed. She screamed just twice, then bit on one knuckle, edged past the body, ran to the ladder shaft.

Pete heard the shot echo throughout the room. The sound galvanized him into effort. He was on his hands and knees when Jan came running to him to throw herself down and put her arms around him.

"Fuller?" Pete croaked.

"Dead," she said.

"We've got to get out of here," he said. He told her, then, what he had done and watched her eyes go wide.

"Oh, no."

"They were going to kill us. I couldn't let them live."

"I understand."

He had noted the time of activation. Less than ten minutes had passed.

"Can you walk?" Jan asked.

"I think so."

He got to his feet and fought the dizziness. A man just didn't get a blow to the head and recover immediately and do heroic things. He walked with his arm across Jan's shoulder for support.

The ladder shaft was torture. He dragged himself up rung by rung, Jan below him, encouraging him. She had not had time to think that her beautiful planet was going to be destroyed. She could think only of Pete, and the fact that they were both alive.

When at last Pete struggled out into the open air the freshness of it seemed to help. They were still a long way, through the undergrowth, from the *Lady Sandy*. The way had been marked as Brad Fuller had hacked away jungle growth. But the going was slow. Pete's head ached, but he was able to keep going. The dizziness came and went.

They broke through into the flood zone, covered by low, rank growth. The *Lady* was there, of course. Pete broke into a staggering run, the growth whipping at his legs.

Inside, breathing hard, fighting to keep from blacking out again, he checked his watch.

"We made it," he said. There was just under an hour left. He could blink the tug far away to safety in mere seconds. The generator was at full charge, all systems operative.

"Pete, isn't there anything we can do?" Jan asked, as he seated himself and began preparations for a quick blink.

"Maybe. If there's time." He'd kept himself on his feet with that hope, that faint, long-shot hope. He'd been thinking of that device down deep in the earth under the old fort. It had been man's last, great achievement in the use of the nuclear fusion. The trigger was a hydrogen bomb. The energy released by the fusion of a light chemical element to form nuclei of heavier elements was relatively minor, exploding so far underground. What happened with that explosion, however, was not minor. The fusion energy triggered an intricate reaction which released the bonding molecular energy of medium-heavy elements with a force which spread and could not be contained, not even by the core and crust of a planet.

The planet buster had been such a terrible weapon that following the war against the Zede II group, a lot of money had been spent finding a way to counter it. There was, of course, no way to stop the reaction once it had been triggered, but U.P. scientists had found a way to disarm a planet buster before the hydrogen trigger exploded. For a long, long time, all ships of the line had been equipped with a magnetic beam which could penetrate miles of solid rock to disrupt the initial fusion action and prevent detonation.

The problem was that when Pete was at the Academy there'd been talk of discontinuing the practice of making the neutralizer mandatory equipment for fleet ships. The chances of *Rimfire*'s having a neutralizer were slim. She was an X&A ship. But X&A ships, going into the unknown, went prepared. Weaponry on an exploratory ship matched, and often exceeded, that of a ship of the line.

He had fifty-two minutes.

He punched in the coordinates for *Rimfire*'s position, and the *Lady Sandy* blinked.

Jan had been busy. She treated the knot on Pete's head, cleaned it, sterilized it. The skin was broken and blood had clotted his hair.

The *Lady* came into normal space a few hundred yards from the shadowy outline of *Rimfire*.

"Get me headache pills," Pete told her. He had some thinking to do. He'd planned how to get into the same never-never zone with *Rimfire* previously, had had it worked out, but he wanted to be sure. Jan was alive, and soft-warm. He wanted to be with her forever, but not frozen in time and space like *Rimfire*.

He took the powerful drug, and his head felt much better almost immediately.

"We need to talk this over, Jan," he said.

"Pete, I don't want to see my planet destroyed."

"It's risky, Jan. We can blink back, call in some of the bright scientists from New Earth. *Rimfire*'s not going anywhere."

"Please," she said.

"It means that much to you?"

"Not if you think it's too risky," she said. "But we were rich, Pete. We had a planet of our own. Didn't you like that?"

"I did."

"I'll leave it up to you."

Forty-nine minutes.

He talked it, using spoken thoughts to get it straight in his mind. "Okay. *Rimfire* programmed a blink in the normal mode. Something, perhaps the size of her generator, the power, something, caused her to vector off onto that generator harmonic which matched the blink mode of ships of a thousand years ago. Her computer was programmed to bring her back into normal space from the normal mode, and didn't function in the altered mode."

She knew what he was doing. He was merely thinking aloud. But the chronometer was ticking off precious seconds.

"The computer says this will work. In effect, I program a mixed blink. If I just programmed a blink in the old mode we'd come back into normal space right past wherever it is that *Rimfire* is hung up. What we have to do is program some delay into the blink, so that we'll exist in the same, whatever, frame, time and space, whatever, that *Rimfire* exists in."

Jan nodded.

"We haven't tried that yet, you know."

"Pete."

"Okay, okay." He punched instructions. "Hang on."

He felt the slide, the exit of his internal organs and tubings. His heart seemed to beat outside of his body, and once again he felt, in that timeless, endless eon of waiting, a great pity for the crew of *Rimfire*.

He'd been looking at Jan's face when he pushed the blink button. If he had to spend eternity frozen in some strange state, he wanted to spend it looking at her.

After a few thousand years, during which he had time to review his entire life, time to remember every moment with Jan, he saw her eyes blink and it was over.

He breathed. "It works."

Thirty-five minutes.

He talked as he made preparations. "What I did was program two sets of exit instructions," he said. "First, the blink was programmed standard-mode, but with the generator tuned old-mode. That left us hung up."

"Wow," Jan said. "I relived my whole life."

"It's not bad, except for that feeling of being outside of one's body," Pete said. "But I also programmed a switch to old mode which, after a delay in tuning the generator—that went on while we were feeling timeless—"

"Evidently doesn't affect a computer," Jan said.

"Evidently not."

So it worked. Now came the ticklish part. He told her what he expected of her. "We're going to have to actually make hull contact with *Rimfire* while we're hung up in time," he said.

That meant a series of tiny blinks. It didn't matter to either the generator or the computer how short the blinks were. The process was the same.

He moved the *Lady Sandy* a few hundred yards closer to the shadow of *Rimfire*, measured carefully. Each blink was the same. Each took an eternity.

"It's almost like psychotherapy," Jan said, as they readied for another small blink which would cut the distance between the ships down to mere feet. "I can go back to the womb. I can remember every sensation, every word I've ever said or read, everything anyone has said to me."

"I spent a few thousand years going over our first month together," Pete said.

He had calculated it carefully. There was no time to wait for the *Lady*'s generator to charge fully.

Twenty-one minutes.

He would make two more of the eternity blinks, hanging in limbo for a time which proved, in real space, to be only seconds. The next-to-the-last blink put the tug's metal side mere inches from the shadowy metal cliff of *Rimfire*'s portside. In normal space it would have been simple. He would merely have snaked a cable over, and the field of the generator would have traveled down the cable to lift *Rimfire* back. However, to exist where *Rimfire* had solidity, he was in a state of frozen time, unable to blink an eye, much less control a cable. It had to be a hull contact. And since no one had ever blinked a ship into actual hull contact he had a few nightmare visions inspired by that man-made sculpture out in deep space, a ship fused, sharing a molecular bone with a stone asteroid.

Nineteen minutes.

Within a few seconds there could very well be another frozen sculpture in space, or in near space, a shadow of two ships, a huge X&A ship and a stubby tug blended together forever and ever, molecules intermixed, flesh become a mixture of metal and all the elements which went into the construction of the two ships.

He used a precious few seconds kissing Jan. She felt, then, her first fear. Until that time she'd had total confidence. The kiss, the way he clung to her, told her that there was, indeed, danger.

"You know," Pete said, releasing her, sitting down, his fingers poised over the blink button, "I've dreamed about this moment from the first day I set foot on a tug. I've envisioned latching onto a big, rich ship. I've repeated a phrase a million times in my mind. Lord, how I'd like to be able to say to this ship, 'Captain, do you accept a Lloyd's?' "

"I know, darling," she said. "I know."

"And here I'm about to latch onto the most expensive, most valuable ship ever built, pull her out of trouble, and I'm not even going to be able to talk."

"It's all right," she said. "We'll have a planet."

If it worked. If *Rimfire* had a neutralizer. If it wasn't already too late.

"Ready?"

"Hold my hand."

He squeezed her hand hard, pushed the button. A metallic, clanging thud was in his ears, remaining there for eons. All of his vital organs, all that was within him, his life force, his everything, seemed to flow up his arm and blend where their flesh made contact with all that was Jan.

12

Captain Dean Richards, having reviewed all he had ever been exposed to in the way of mathematics, amused himself for a few thousand years figuring exactly how far his hand had moved. He'd started it toward his forehead to brush back his hair a few eternities past and it had moved exactly .0000000 0001211 millimeters. It would be interesting to calculate, in units of near infinity, how long he'd feel the tickle of the lock of hair.

Tiring of that, Richards began at the beginning again. He knew the first moment of sensation. He was in the womb. He could feel the thump-thump of his mother's heart, hear the singing sound of blood in his tiny, forming veins.

After a few times through a lifetime, things were revealed which had been lost in the haste or excitement of the moment in actual life. He found that he could concentrate on things he had seen with peripheral vision only and create almost a new set of lifetime awareness.

The brain was, he had found, a most marvelous organ. He was astounded by the things it had stored, things which he hadn't even noticed at the time.

Lord, what an educational tool! He could review, word by word, thought by thought, every book he'd ever read. He could extend theory. He was a mental superman, but he was helpless.

And then the damned ship's alarm system clanged and clanged and Julie Rainbow was looking up at him with wide eyes.

"Object in hull contact, sir," Julie said.

He had not fully recovered. He was still living an interesting, forgotten segment of his life. And things were happening too fast. The alarm was clanging and people were leaping to stations and a voice came at him from the bulkheads and all the metal in the ship.

"Captain," the voice said, "do you accept a Lloyd's?"

"What in holy hell?" Dean Richards said.

13

He had to say it. He just had to say it. He'd just undergone an eternity of closeness with Jan which was unlike any other experience of his life, their souls, everything that was them blended and aware at the point of contact, their closely held hands. And he'd lived his life again, knew that with the knowledge he'd accumulated in deep, word-by-word study of every book he'd ever read he could breeze through any exam the Academy could throw at him and then teach the professors a thing or two.

All that, and he still had to say, "Captain, do you accept a Lloyd's?"

He sent the question through the cable communications system and it reverberated in the hull of the *Lady*. Then he clicked on the voice communicator.

"Identify," *Rimfire* sent.

"U.P.S tug *Ramco Lady Sandy*," Pete said.

"This is Captain Dean Richards, *U.P.S. Rimfire*. I see no reason to understand your question."

"You did seconds or eternities ago, Captain," Pete said.

Dean Richards brushed the lock of hair back from his forehead. Yes, the man was right. But now *Rimfire* was functioning perfectly.

"Captain Richards," Pete said, "we can talk about that later. This is a vital question. Do you have a planet-buster neutralizer on board?"

Richards was still trying to clear his head. "That, sir, is service business, not yours," he said.

Fifteen minutes.

Pete's fingers flew. He felt the strange, eerie tug, knew that suspended, timeless feeling. He passed it going over the little he'd ever read about planet busters and neutralizers. Then they were back in normal space again.

"Captain Richards," he said, "you have an empty generator." He was angry. Seconds were ticking away. Jan's beautiful planet was just under fourteen minutes away from destruction. "You can't blink. Answer my question or I'll blink you back and leave you there until I can get messages back to New Earth and get a fleet ship out here."

"That is classified information," Richards said.

"My God, man, a planet's going to blow up," Pete shouted into the communicator. "I can explain everything later."

"Yes, we have a neutralizer."

"How long will it take to get it activated and to do the job?"

"Hold one," Richards said.

Paul Victor, rubbing his eyes in puzzlement, had come into the control room. Richards put the question to him.

"Activate in two minutes," Paul said. "In position,

five minutes to do the job. Maybe a little more if there's a great deal of heavy metal in the planet's crust."

"Get it going," Richards said. He'd let the whole exchange be broadcast to the tug which was in hull contact with the *Rimfire*. Even as he gave the order he felt the *Rimfire* blink. The tug had moved him. More alarms sounded. He checked visuals and saw a water planet quite close.

Ten minutes.

"The buster is immediately under the fortified position directly below," Pete said. "We have nine minutes and twenty seconds and counting."

Paul Victor looked up quickly. He'd started warming the neutralizer. It had one minute and thirty seconds to go before it was ready. He spoke into the communicator. "Young man," he said, "it's going to be close. I'd suggest that you be prepared to blink us to hell out of here."

"Just neutralize that thing," Pete said.

"Neutralizer activated," Paul said.

Pete looked at the chronometer. Six minutes, thirty seconds. Jan was at his side, tense, her hand on his shoulder, her eyes on the visuals to get, she felt, what might be her last look at her beautiful planet. She'd seen Pete punch in a blink coordinate. She knew that he was ready to blink both ships out of the range of the devastating explosion.

"There's a planet buster down there, all right," Paul Victor said, as he sent the neutralizing beam out and down to flash through the planet's crust. "And there's one hell of a lot of heavy metal."

He had six minutes and five seconds to kill the capacity to react in a hydrogen warhead.

"It will be very, very close," Paul said.

"Keep the tug skipper posted," Richards told him.

"It's old," Paul said, "but it's alive. Good, strong reading. Going down slowly."

Jan reached for Pete's hand, praying at the same time. She was careful not to hold the hand which was poised over the blink button. There was just enough charge left in the *Lady*'s generator to lift both ships to safety.

Four minutes. Three. Two. At sixty seconds, Pete began to count down.

"*Lady Sandy,*" Paul Victor said, "we're not going to make it. I'm sorry."

"Forty-nine," Pete counted. "Forty-eight."

He'd lost it all. No Lloyd's on the *Rimfire*. No planet. And one hell of a lot of explaining to do.

"Fusion potential coming down," Paul said tensely, watching the clock, hearing the tug captain's countdown.

"Thirty," Pete counted. "Twenty-nine."

"Get us out of here," Dean Richards said. "Now."

"Twenty-five. Twenty-f—" He jerked to attention, his finger jabbing at the blink button at the same time. The damned thing had gone off early. He saw it clearly, saw it in full Tri-D color on the viewer, saw the old fortification tremble and buckle upward, and as his finger hit the blink button and the viewer went black he saw just a beginning burst of fire dissolve the domed roof of the fort.

"We lost it all, honey," he said, the ship back in normal space.

"*Lady Sandy*, where are we?" Dean Richards asked.

Rimfire's computer was working. He'd have coordinates within seconds, but his viewers showed nothingness, blackness.

Pete, in a dull voice, gave *Rimfire* the coordinates of the position. He'd blinked back to the midpoint beacon, back toward the galaxy and the New Earth range. He felt drained. His head hurt. With all the renewed knowledge in his head he couldn't imagine how he'd explain all of the events of the past few hours to a service inquiry board. They'd have a ball with just one aspect of it, how he and Jan came to be in command of the *Ramco Lady Sandy*. All the proof, all the evidence, was flying outward from a central point in fragments and molten lava.

No planet. No salvage contract. No job.

He stood, pulled Jan into his arms. He had that. Yes, he had that.

"Sir," the voice said on the communicator, "I'd like to know your name."

Pete gave it.

"Captain Jaynes," Richards said, "we're beginning to piece things together a bit over here. I have many questions. I'd like to suggest that you suit up and enter *Rimfire* through the hatch just astern of you."

It was, Pete knew, not a suggestion. It was an order. He wasn't about to go anywhere without Jan. They suited up.

The cold of space is a tangible thing. It can crystallize metal. It can make itself felt through the best-insulated spacesuit, if only psychologically. They moved along the *Lady*'s hull clinging to safety lines, magnetic shoes clomping on the hull. Line at his waist, Pete pushed himself, floating, from the *Lady*'s stern, contacted the hull of the *Rimfire* feet-first, pulled Jan across.

Two efficient service ratings helped them out of their suits once the airlock had filled, led them forward to the control room. All of *Rimfire*'s officers were congregated there. Julie Rainbow was at her post.

Pete accepted the outstretched hand of the *Rimfire*'s captain, introduced Jan, shook hands with the other officers.

"Well," Pete said, feeling very, very tired, "there's a lot of explaining to do."

Richards smiled, waved them to a seat. "I think we already have a few of the answers, Captain." Rimfire's crew had been working during the period of time it took Pete and Jan to cross over and enter the X&A ship.

"I want to confirm one thing, first," Richards said. "May I look at your watch?"

Pete's wristwatch was standard service issue. He held his arm out, crooking his wrist so that Richards could see the face.

Richards whistled and help up his own wrist, but Pete had already checked the control-room chronometer.

"Captain," Richards said, "in view of this I think we can have a little talk, later, about that Lloyd's contract you mentioned. My engineer, Mr. Victor, tells me that some abnormality in our generator got us caught up in subspace. Is that your opinion?"

"Captain," Pete said, "it's a long story, and I'll be happy to tell it to you. I have only one request. Well, two. First, we'd love a cup of good service coffee, and I'd like your word that you'll listen to the entire thing before you start asking questions. It seems that all the proof of what is going to seem like a bunch of wild lies went up with our planet."

Julie Rainbow was already in motion. She had two steaming mugs of coffee within seconds.

"You said your planet," Richards prompted, as Pete sipped.

"Captain," Julie Rainbow said, "excuse me."

Richards looked at her with one raised eyebrow. The girl was never going to learn not to interrupt. It seemed ages ago and only days ago that he'd told her—

"Captain," Julie persisted, "that planet. It's still there."

Jan leaped to her feet.

Julie nodded. "I just put the long-range detectors on it." *Rimfire*'s detectors were vastly superior to the detectors on board a tug. "I wanted to see what a planet buster did, and it's still there."

Jan had spilled coffee when she leaped to her feet. It didn't matter. She put her mug down and started doing a little dance of joy. She pulled Pete to his feet and hugged him.

"It's still there," she whispered. "It's still there."

"Captain," Pete said, "before I start talking, can we check out Jan's Planet visually? What's on that planet will answer a lot of questions."

"I don't want to risk a blink with the *Rimfire*, not until I know what the hell happened," Richards said.

Pete turned to the computer, and even as Richards started to protest, his fingers flew. "It's all right. I'll explain later. It's a simple matter of tuning the generator. I didn't take time to do that. I just programmed instruction." And with that, even as Paul Victor lunged at him, he pressed the blink button, and they all froze, felt the eerie, old mode, and were back in space within visual of a beautiful blue-and-white water world, one of the most beautiful sights in the universe, a life-zone planet.

"There was a nuclear blast," Paul Victor said, after examining instruments. "Either it was too weak to trigger the buster, or the buster malfunctioned."

There was a crater at the site of the old fort, edges glazed by heat. There'd been some radiation released into the air, but nothing which would give anyone any problems. The site of the explosion itself could be cleared by an antiradiation team in a couple of months.

"And now, young man," Paul Victor said, "I want to know what you meant when you said something about tuning a generator."

"I have some questions first," Richards said.

"I think they'll all be answered as I go through it," Pete said, grinning down at an ecstatic Jan. "Two things first."

"Coffee?" Julie Rainbow asked, coming to her feet.

"Yes, thank you," Pete said. "Then I'll record our claim to the planet on the *Rimfire*'s permanent tapes, just to make it doubly offical."

"And then maybe you'll be kind enough to tell us what the hell has been happening," Richards said.

"Be glad to, sir," Pete said, unable to control the grin, feeling Jan at his side, soft-warm and wonderful.

14

The atmospace yacht *Jan's Planet,* cleared for approach and landing at Rimfire Spaceport, zapped down with a flair, leveling and stopping just before disastrous impact seemed imminent. She skimmed the pad, settled in front of a large, private hangar. White-clad attendants swarmed around her as the hatch opened. Directly behind her a service launch made a more sedate approach, a slow, careful landing, eased to come to rest near the *Jan's Planet.* Again the white-clad attendants scurried.

They met halfway between the ships, a rather handsome foursome, a fleet admiral in service blue, a fleet captain, dainty, pretty even in the severe uniform, and a sportily dressed couple who came from *Jan's Planet* hand in hand.

Captain Julie Rainbow ran a few steps forward to kiss first Jan, then Pete. Dean Richards, his temples showing a bit of distinguished gray, embraced Jan and shook Pete's hand. The four boarded *Jan's Planet.* Pete had given the crew time off, so there were just the four of them as the sleek yacht soared vertically and then leveled and shot into the stratosphere and into near space on a ballistic trajectory.

"Good Lord," Julie laughed, as the trajectory peaked and she felt that over-the-hump quick kiss of momentary weightlessness. "That's the first time I've done that since I was a kid in trainers."

"Pete's in his second childhood," Jan said.

"Nothing too good for real heroes," Pete said. "First to circumnavigate the galaxy, discoverers of humpteen new life-zone planets."

Dean Richards was using the visuals. "Richardsville has grown," he said.

"Namesake of the principal city on Jan's Planet," Pete went on. "Want me to do the kiss-me-quick again?"

"I came here to see a museum," Dean Richards said.

"Don't let him kid you," Julie said. "He came to see the city named after him and to see his godson."

"How is little Dean?" Richards asked.

"Pete's ready to buy him his first ship," Jan laughed.

"Well, he's smart for a five-year-old," Pete said.

He was going down, calling for clearance. The skies of Jan's Planet were no longer theirs and theirs alone. He made one of the patented, wild, heart-stopping Jaynes landings. A ground vehicle wheeled up to the yacht. As the four boarded, Julie admired the building ahead. It was set in the center of a vast, deeply grassed plain.

"You picked a spot for it, all right," she said.

The ground vehicle delivered them to an impressive entrance under a sign which said: JAYNES MUSEUM OF ANCIENT WEAPONS OF WAR.

Pete and Dean fell behind as the tour of the new museum began. The curator hired by Pete, noting that the two men seemed to want to talk, directed his comments to Jan and Julie.

"You made a wise decision, Pete," Richards said, "taking the finder's fee in land."

"I didn't think so the first few years," Pete said.

"That mining contract on the eastern desert didn't hurt you."

"Nope."

"Hope you're seeing to it that they don't mess up the land."

"Sure," Pete said. "It's a clean operation, all underground. There's the same desert up above that was there when we first saw it."

A flash of memory. Jan's Planet in his viewers for the first time, the loss of the old *Stranden 47*, the terrible moment when he'd seen nuclear fire burn up through the domed roof of the old fort on South America. He'd named the continents of the western hemisphere after similar landmasses on old Earth. The first few years of residence on one of their vast tracts of land on the continent he'd named North America. And, not quite so pleasant, the months of investigations which had finally resulted in confirmation of their claim to the planet, and to the salvage contract on *U.P.S. Rimfire.* Favorable testimony by Dean Richards and his officers had helped, and a firm friendship had resulted.

"Guess you've heard that the Academy and the service are now using old-mode hangup time for pounding education into the heads of empty-headed cadets," Richards said.

"Read something about it." He halted in front of a battered, partly melted tug. The *47*, lifted from the eastern desert, had a permanent home in the museum.

"Pete, I'm always pleased when we can stop off here, but I made a special trip this time," Richards said.

Pete turned, brought his mind back from the sweet, sweet days aboard that old Mule of a tug.

"Department of Space and Alien Exploration suggested it," Richards said. "You've made yourself quite a reputation with those papers on theoretical effects of blink-generator tunings."

"Ummm," Pete said.

"They've assigned me to research your theory that the pre-blink signal can be read both ways."

"Good," Pete said. "I'll be glad to see some work done on that." It needed someone with the power of deductive reasoning, he felt. An old Academy kick-out could only take it so far, reasoning that although subspace has dimension, of sorts, that that dimension is infinitely large or small and that there should be a way to take the short way to infinity, read the emergence of a pre-blink signal and use that signal to make blinks into previously unexplored space. By doing so, the long, tedious exploration to lay new blink routes would be eliminated.

"X&A has authorized me to offer you a temporary admiralcy," Dean said.

Pete's fingers went to his skull, played there for only a second. "What in the hell for?"

"To be consultant on the project. We'll use Julie's ship, the old *Rimfire*. I'll be project boss."

Lord, Lord, he was thinking. Admiral Peter Jaynes. He laughed.

"Intrigues you, doesn't it?" Richards asked.

"It does." If it had come a few years earlier he would have leaped at it.

"Like to have you and Jan aboard."

"Dean, I wish to hell I could."

"Thinking about little Dean?"

"Yeah. We're away from him enough as it is. And we've just started renovation of the fort in the desert. It's the best-preserved one. Give people a chance to see the kind of things men did back when we fought wars. And we've got our first crop of wheat coming up out on the plains."

"Well," Richards said, "I told them I wouldn't be able to pry you away."

"I'm afraid not. You'll keep me posted, I hope."

"Sure. Might be calling on you for some of that nondeductive reasoning of yours, too. You know what it will mean if you're right about this."

He knew. A ship could move through space, through any space, in galaxy or out, just as fast as the blink charge would build. No more careful probes to be sure blink lines were clear. Julie Rainbow, for example, could take the *Rimfire* out past the periphery, send an exploratory pre-blink signal, clear the area, and be on the fringe of another galaxy in one blink.

"Well, our ladies are waiting," Richards said.

A quick, low orbit of the planet showed the two service officers how well settlement and development were going, and then they were on the launch headed back for *Rimfire*.

The sleek atmospace yacht blinked outward, past *Rimfire*, even as she pointed her blink signal for the familiar blackness of intergalactic space.

Jan's Planet headed inward, hit the New Earth

range, and blinked to come to rest in normal space near blink beacon NE795.

Nearby, a Stranden Mule kept vigil over the junction of blink routes. The two-man crew, man and wife, had a few moments of interest in a boring, three-year hitch as the pre-blink signal of the yacht came and a brief courtesy greeting was exchanged. The man-wife, with four months to go to relief, were dreaming of a holiday back on Tigian.

"Every year, same time," the tugboat man told his wife.

"New yacht this time," the wife said.

"Same name."

"Yes."

The man adjusted the visuals to have the yacht in view. "Every year same thing. They say hello and then put up a privacy screen. I wonder what the hell they do over there for two weeks same time every year?"

Jan came into the lounge on board *Jan's Planet* in a silken singlet. "Ready for coffee?" she asked.

"Sounds good," Pete said.

She poured. He sighed in contentment. Two weeks. Two glorious weeks of nothing. Nothing but Jan. Little Dean was in good hands living it up on the farms. Two glorious weeks. She looked more like a Tri-D star than a girl he'd talked away from the Spacer's Rest, Lord, how many years ago?

"You'd like to be out there with Dean and Julie, wouldn't you?" Jan asked, as she sat beside him and he felt the silken touch of her hip against his.

"In a way. But not now. This is my time."

"And, sir, your time is my time," she said.

"Sure you don't think this is a dull way to spend a vacation?"

"What do you think?"

His fingers went to his skull. She reached for his hand. "I'll tell you what I think," she said. She said it with silent, moist, pressing lips.

ABOUT THE AUTHOR

ZACH HUGHES is the pen name of Hugh Zachary, who, with his wife Elizabeth, runs a book factory in North Carolina. Hugh quit a timeclock job in 1963 and turned to writing full-time. He is the author of a number of well-received science fiction novels, and together with Elizabeth, he has turned out many fine historical romances, as well as books in half a dozen other fields.

Hugh Zachary has worked in radio and tv broadcasting and as a newspaper feature writer. He has also been a carpenter, run a charter fishing boat, done commercial fishing, and served as a mate on an anchor-handling tugboat in the North Sea oil fields.

Hugh's science fiction novels, KILLBIRD, PRESSURE MAN, and THUNDERWORLD are available in Signet editions.

SIGNET Science Fiction You'll Enjoy

(0451)

- ☐ **SIDESHOW (Tales of the Galactic Midway #1) by Mike Resnick.** (118480—$2.50)*
- ☐ **THE THREE-LEGGED HOOTCH DANCER (Tales of the Galactic Midway #2) by Mike Resnick.** (120825—$2.50)*
- ☐ **THE WILD ALIEN TAMER (Tales of the Galactic Midway #3) by Mike Resnick.** (123905—$2.50)*
- ☐ **THE BEST ROOTIN' TOOTIN' SHOOTIN' GUNSLINGER IN THE WHOLE DAMNED GALAXY (Tales of the Galactic Midway #4) by Mike Resnick.** (125231—$2.50)*
- ☐ **WALPURGIS III by Mike Resnick.** (115724—$2.25)
- ☐ **BIRTHRIGHT: THE BOOK OF MAN by Mike Resnick.** (113586—$2.75)
- ☐ **THE SOUL EATER by Mike Resnick.** (110927—$2.25)
- ☐ **DANCER'S ILLUSION by Ann Maxwell.** (124618—$2.50)*
- ☐ **DANCER'S LUCK by Ann Maxwell.** (122534—$2.50)*
- ☐ **FIRE DANCER by Ann Maxwell.** (119398—$2.50)*
- ☐ **THE JAWS OF MENX by Ann Maxwell.** (110374—$2.75)
- ☐ **EYES OF AMBER AND OTHER STORIES by Joan D. Vinge.** (120833—$2.75)*
- ☐ **OUTCASTS OF HEAVEN BELT by Joan D. Vinge.** (116534—$2.50)*
- ☐ **A RUMOR OF ANGELS by Marge B. Kellogg.** (123484—$2.50)*

*Prices slightly higher in Canada

Buy them at your local bookstore or use this convenient coupon for ordering.

THE NEW AMERICAN LIBRARY, INC.,
P.O. Box 999, Bergenfield, New Jersey 07621

Please send me the books I have checked above. I am enclosing $__________
(please add $1.00 to this order to cover postage and handling). Send check or money order—no cash or C.O.D.'s. Prices and numbers are subject to change without notice.

Name____________________

Address____________________

City __________ State __________ Zip Code __________

Allow 4-6 weeks for delivery.
This offer is subject to withdrawal without notice.

TREK®

The Magazine For Star Trek Fans

Did you enjoy reading this collection selected from the Best of TREK, The Magazine For Star Trek Fans? If so, then you will want to start reading TREK regularly! In addition to the same type of features, articles, and artwork in this collection, each issue of TREK features dozens of photos of your Star Trek favorites – all beautifully halftoned for the finest possible reproduction! TREK has full-color front and back covers, is fully typeset, and is printed on high-quality coated paper destined to last a lifetime! In short, TREK is the finest Star Trek magazine available today, at any price. Remember, if you aren't reading TREK, then you are missing half the fun of being a Star Trek fan! So order a copy of our current issue today – or better yet, subscribe, and be sure of never missing an issue!

Current issue .... $3.50 plus 50 cents postage
4 issue subscription $13.00
8 issue subscription $26.00
4 issue subscription (Canada) $14.00
8 issue subscription (Canada) $28.00

TREK PUBLICATIONS

1120 Omar .... Houston, Texas 77009